Ruby grinned. "Are you flirting with me?"

Heath looked at her. "Of course. You're so beautiful it'd be stupid for me not to."

Her heart pounded frantically. She was painfully aware of every breath. "You're not half bad yourself."

"Now who's the flirt?"

She shrugged. "I learned from the best."

"Me? Am I the best?"

"Believe it or not, you are."

It felt as though she was perched on the edge of a cliff and something was telling her to jump. In truth, all she wanted was a kiss. It had been so long since she'd kissed a man, since she'd been able to get lost in someone. But was she ready for that? Logic said that three years was more than enough time. But that was the funny thing about loss—logic didn't matter. It was all up to the heart.

And right now, her heart and body wanted Heath.

* * *

Rancher After Midnight by Karen Booth
is part of the Texas Cattleman's Club:
Ranchers and Rivals series.

Dear Reader,

Welcome back to Royal, Texas! I'm so excited for you to read my contribution to the Ranchers and Rivals season—*Rancher After Midnight*! This is an emotional romance, jam-packed with redemption.

Hero Heath Thurston has been hated by nearly everyone in Royal for the entirety of this series. People think he's mean, vindictive and motivated by money, but the truth behind Heath's motivation is far from being that simple. Unfortunately, he hides his true feelings from everyone, including himself.

Ruby Rose Bennett is our heroine, a woman who's had to overcome her own unfortunate history. From the very first words of this story, I felt it in my heart that these two needed each other. But how would they figure it out? Could Heath put aside his pride to see that? And could Ruby open herself up to love? Those are the questions...and I hope you enjoy the answers!

Drop me a line anytime at karen@karenbooth.net and let me know if you enjoyed *Rancher After Midnight*. I love hearing from readers!

Karen

KAREN BOOTH

RANCHER AFTER MIDNIGHT

Special thanks and acknowledgment are given
to Karen Booth for her contribution to the
Texas Cattleman's Club: Ranchers and Rivals miniseries.

Recycling programs
for this product may
not exist in your area.

ISBN-13: 978-1-335-58156-3

Rancher After Midnight

Copyright © 2022 by Harlequin Enterprises ULC

For questions and comments about the quality of this book, please contact us at CustomerService@Harlequin.com.

Harlequin Enterprises ULC
22 Adelaide St. West, 41st Floor
Toronto, Ontario M5H 4E3, Canada
www.Harlequin.com

Printed in U.S.A.

Karen Booth is a Midwestern girl transplanted in the South, raised on '80s music and repeated readings of *Forever...* by Judy Blume. When she takes a break from the art of romance, she's listening to music with her college-age kids or sweet-talking her husband into making her a cocktail. Learn more about Karen at karenbooth.net.

Books by Karen Booth

Harlequin Desire

Blue Collar Billionaire
Rancher After Midnight

Little Black Book of Secrets

The Problem with Playboys
Black Tie Bachelor Bid
How to Fake a Wedding Date

The Sterling Wives

Once Forbidden, Twice Tempted
High Society Secrets
All He Wants for Christmas

Visit her Author Profile page at Harlequin.com, or karenbooth.net, for more titles.

You can also find Karen Booth on Facebook, along with other Harlequin Desire authors, at Facebook.com/harlequindesireauthors!

For my fellow Harlequin Desire authors
and the editorial team at Harlequin.
You make me feel like a member of
the coolest romance club ever!

One

The entire population of Royal, Texas, thought Heath Thurston was a bullheaded jerk. Or at least it seemed that way. They talked about him like he was a mean dog with a bone. A veritable thorn in everyone's side. Heath did not care. Not one whit. They could call him names until they were blue in the face. He wasn't about to let go of his mission, especially not on account of public opinion. If he had to scrap and fight until his dying breath, he'd have some semblance of justice for his mother, Cynthia, and half sister, Ashley. They were no longer on this earth to fight for themselves. And no one else seemed to care that they'd both been wronged while they were alive.

Even his twin brother, Nolan, was shrugging off

what the Grandins and Lattimores, two of the biggest and most powerful families in the town, had done to Cynthia and Ashley. *Let it go*, Nolan had said. *It's time to move on.* But that was easy for Nolan to say. He'd hardly been around at all over the last fifteen years after heading off for greener pastures and leaving Heath to take care of everything at home. Sure, Nolan had finally returned to Royal, but that was only to turn around and be blinded by love—the love of a Grandin, no less. Chelsea. The woman he'd married. Heath could hardly believe the state of affairs. Nine months ago, he'd started his crusade against the Grandin and Lattimore families. And now he was related by marriage to one of them.

To make things worse, it was snowing. "What in the hell is going on?" he muttered under his breath. He peered out the windshield of his Ford F-150 Limited, a truck that was tough as nails on the outside and pure luxury inside. This was not typical weather for Royal, not even a few days after Christmas. It had never occurred to him to check the forecast before he headed out to Ruby Rose Bennett's house so he could talk to her about the oil survey she'd done on the Grandin and Lattimore properties. Her report's ultimate finding was "inconclusive," which Heath found unacceptable. An old report had said there wasn't oil, but he didn't trust it. So either there was oil on that land or there wasn't, and it was her job to find the answer. If there was oil, his mother and half sister had been entitled to it when they were alive. Since they were no longer here to fight for themselves, Heath was going to have to continue to do it for them on his own.

He would not fail. Even though he could admit to himself that things were looking bleak, he was also sure that he was not out of chances. He still had a few cards tucked up his sleeve. And he hoped that Ruby Rose Bennett might be able to help him play a winning hand.

His GPS told him that her driveway was ahead on the right, so he slowed down and made the turn. He was well beyond the city limits of Royal, out in a quiet rural area where there weren't many homes visible from the road and the parcels of land were vast. He started up the winding gravel road and drove up and over the crest of a hill, then began crawling along through a stand of trees that became more dense with every passing minute. He had to wonder what Ruby Rose Bennett was doing living this far out, in such an isolated and remote location. Perhaps she was a loner.

He'd never met the woman, but he imagined her to be in her late fifties or early sixties, possibly with a head of gray hair. Land surveyor was a rugged vocation, especially in Texas, where the terrain could be as unforgiving as it was beautiful. *Surveyor* conjured images of an ornery old man, so he could only envision that a woman in that line of work might have a similar aesthetic. Her email address, their main mode of communication, tipped him off to her age as well, since it suggested someone who did not keep pace with technology. The final hint had been their one phone call. Ruby Rose had a gruff voice that made her sound like a woman who'd been through a lot. He could relate. He'd been through the wringer as well.

The snow seemed to be coming down faster with every passing minute. It really was the most bizarre sight. Heath had lived in Royal his entire life and could count on one hand the number of times they'd had this sort of winter weather. He tried to take it as an omen that things were changing. Hopefully, that included his luck. He was tired of battling the Grandins and the Lattimores. He wanted them to turn over what they'd promised so he could begin the process of moving on in his life. What that might look like, however, he wasn't sure.

Eventually, he spotted the house he presumed to belong to Ms. Bennett. A paved driveway led him to the cute and tidy cottage, painted deep blue with crisp white trim, a high-pitched roof and a stone foundation. Window boxes sat at the sills of leaded-glass panes, overflowing with Christmas greenery of cedar, pine and holly, which now had a frosty coating of fresh snow. Perhaps old Ruby Rose Bennett kept herself busy during her leisure time by decorating for the holidays.

He parked his car off to the far right side, near a

cluster of tall trees he hoped would shield his vehicle from any heavy accumulation of snow. He killed the engine and climbed out, bracing for the icy air. He stuffed his hands into his coat pockets and marched up the steps and onto her front porch, his cowboy boots thumping on the wide decking boards. Heath knocked on her door, which was adorned with a rather elaborate holiday wreath. After several moments, there was no answer, but he could see a light on inside, so he knocked again. *Must be taking her some time to get here.* Perhaps that was the problem with the survey Ruby Rose had done. She might not be as able-bodied as the job required. If that was the case, he'd have to find someone else to do it.

When the door finally opened, it felt as though the air was knocked right out of his lungs. Before him stood a stunning woman. Scratch that—she was drop-dead gorgeous. She was tall and willowy, with wavy blond hair, bright green eyes and full pink lips that, unfortunately, weren't saying a thing.

"Yes. Uh, hello." He glanced down at his feet, just to take a breather from her considerable beauty. "I'm looking for Ruby Rose Bennett. Is she home?"

"You're Heath Thurston, aren't you?" The woman eyed him up and down, making him incredibly self-conscious. And if he was being honest, a little turned on. Still, he was taken aback by the fact that she knew who he was. Had his reputation preceded him?

"That's me. I hired Ms. Bennett to do some sur-

vey work for me and I need to speak to her about it."
He peered into the foyer for some sign of Ruby Rose.

"Okay. Although, I'm hardly dressed to discuss business." The woman looked down at herself. She was wearing a white sweater that hung off her shoulder, revealing a particularly enticing stretch of very touchable skin. Her somewhat beat-up blue jeans fit her like a glove. "A call or an email to set up a meeting would've been nice."

"Wait. What?" It felt as though his brain was fighting him as he struggled to reconcile his assumptions about Ruby Rose Bennett's appearance and the reality of the person standing before him. "You're Ruby Rose?"

"Most people call me Ruby. Add in the Rose and it sounds a little old-fashioned. Although, there's nothing wrong with that, and I do like the name. It was my mother's."

Heath wanted to laugh at how he'd jumped to the wrong conclusion about her. He was normally on the mark when summing up people. This time, he'd been more than a little off base. "Okay, then, Ruby. We need to talk."

"And as I just said, a call or an email would've been nice. At the very least, a text."

"I did call. And email you."

"When, exactly?"

Heath did not appreciate her attitude. He had a

legitimate reason to be here. "Yesterday. And this morning."

"It's Saturday. Two days after Christmas. I take time off at the holidays, Mr. Thurston. Curl up with a good book. Drink a mug of hot cocoa. Maybe even with a shot of rum in it. Relax. Perhaps you should try it."

Heath narrowed his vision on her. Dammit, she was pretty, but he did not like the words coming out of her mouth, or more specifically, the condescension with which she delivered them. "I don't need a lesson in how to conduct myself, Ms. Bennett. I hired you to survey the Grandin and Lattimore properties for oil, and I'm not happy with the results. 'Inconclusive' is not an answer."

"I'm sorry about that, but just like the sun coming up in the morning, I have no control over some things. Either Mother Nature spent millions of years creating crude oil on that property, or she didn't. And although I'd love to give you the exact answer, the terrain doesn't allow for it unless you want to spend a whole lot more money."

"More money? You haven't given me what I paid for in the first place, which is a yes or no answer."

"Unfortunately, it's not as simple as that." As if Mother Nature herself was on Ruby's side in this argument, a fierce and bitter wind whipped over Heath's shoulders and straight into her foyer. She wrapped her arms around her midsection. "My gut is to tell you to go home, Mr. Thurston, but with the weather the way it is, you should come inside if you still want to talk about this."

Heath didn't appreciate that her inclination was to send him on his way, but he was thankful she was willing to reconsider. "Yes. That would be great. Thank you." He stepped inside and stomped his feet on the rug.

"Take your boots off."

"I'd prefer to keep them on, if it's all the same to you." Heath didn't walk around in his socks, especially not in front of a beautiful woman when they were about to discuss business.

"Well, it's not all the same to me."

"Excuse me?"

"Have you ever refinished wood floors, Mr. Thurston? By yourself? By *hand*?" She punctuated her question with an artful arch of her eyebrow.

"No."

"Well, I have, and I don't intend to undo my hard work. So take off your boots. Please."

"I'm not staying for long."

She laughed quietly, shaking her head. "You are exactly as bullheaded as everyone says you are, aren't you?"

There it was. Ruby Rose Bennett was on the same side as the rest of Royal. Like everyone else, she thought his stubbornness was a flaw in his personality. When in truth, it was only out of love and a thirst for justice that he was on this crusade. "If that's what you want to call it, then sure. I am."

Ruby was sure of one thing—Heath wasn't going to take off his boots no matter how hard she argued with him. She'd seen Heath's type before. He was rich and entitled, and wound entirely too tight as a result. She had little admiration for any of those qualities, but in his case, she sure could appreciate the appealing package they came wrapped up in. He was temptingly tall, a good five or six inches on her, just enough of an advantage to make her raise her chin and take notice. His hair was touchable and thick and such a dark brown that it was like night, set off by a pair of the most intense and stormy eyes she'd ever seen. For the first time in years, her pulse quickened because of a man. Did that mean she was finally coming back to life? After the loss she'd endured, she'd had every reason to believe she never would.

Despite Heath being a serious case of eye candy, she had to wonder if it had been a mistake to take a job from him. The first whiff of trouble came the day she'd gone out to the Grandin and Lattimore properties to do his survey and she was stopped by a man she knew to be Vic Grandin. Vic had been deeply suspicious of her presence. Enough to make her uncomfortable. Days later at the Royal Diner, she overheard some chatter about a paternity saga in the Grandin family. She didn't have many ties to Royal, but people talked, and this seemed to be a big topic of conversation. She'd heard some real mouthfuls about Heath, too, about his greed and vindictiveness. Was her assignment really about finding oil? Or was there something else at play? She didn't like getting mixed up in other people's affairs.

"Can I get you anything to drink?" Ruby asked as she led Heath down the hall to her living room and kitchen, an open and airy space she'd created when she knocked down the wall between the two rooms soon after buying this cottage three years ago.

"I'm good."

"You sure? Something hot, like coffee? It's not long before dinnertime, but I'm happy to put on a pot."

He shook his head. "I think it's best if we discuss business, so I can leave you to the rest of your day."

As much as she enjoyed looking at him, perhaps this was for the best. "I don't think the weather's supposed to improve anytime soon, so probably a good idea. What do you want to know?"

"I don't see how 'inconclusive' is an acceptable result from an oil survey. Either there's oil or there isn't."

"As I said when I answered the door, it's not that simple, especially in this part of Texas. There are trace amounts of oil almost everywhere. As for the Grandin and Lattimore properties, I did my best with the budget you provided."

"What does that mean?"

"It means that I did what the fee allowed for. I examined any and all surface rock formations. Most contained shale, which can sometimes indicate the presence of oil. Then I did low-level seismic readings, which produced zero evidence of oil. Hence the term 'inconclusive.' It was all in my report."

He pressed his lips together tightly. "Which is more reliable? The rocks or the readings?"

"The readings. By far."

He grimaced. "Are they ever wrong?"

"No. But not all seismic tests are created equal." She wandered around to the other side of her kitchen island, which acted as a natural separation in the great room, and grabbed the mug of cocoa she'd been drinking before he arrived. She took a sip. It was lukewarm, but still delicious, a recipe she'd perfected in the last few years. "If you want to know with one hundred percent confidence, we would need to bring in some serious heavy machinery and do some blasting. We're talking tens of thousands of dollars, or more, and a lot of time. I'm happy to do it if that's what you want." Despite her reticence, she'd take a second job from him. Or a third. Money was tight. "That is, after you convince the families to let you do it."

"I have the deed to the oil in my possession. It gives me the right to do whatever I want on that land in order to get to what's below the surface. And I can sell those rights to an oil company tomorrow. They can start bringing in drills right away."

"I hate to break this to you, Mr. Thurston, but no oil company is going to buy those rights without first verifying the presence of what they're after. And from the available evidence, I doubt you'd be able to get them interested." She'd dealt plenty with oil companies. She knew how they worked and they most certainly did not throw their money away on useless land. "Plus, the Grandin and Lattimore homesteads are beautiful. You really want to go out there and start tearing them up? For nothing?"

He dismissed her comment with a toss of his head. "Maybe that's what they deserve."

Now, *that* sounded like a grudge. Heath wasn't a particularly sympathetic man. He was gruff and quick to make assumptions. Still, there was a part of her that felt for him. He seemed desperate, with a serious case of tunnel vision, both of which could make a person do unreasonable things. "I assume you know about the original survey of the land years ago. There was zero evidence of oil."

"You saw that?"

"I did. I went back and looked up any old surveys after I completed mine. I don't like the word *inconclusive* any more than you do. I wanted to be sure I hadn't missed anything."

"Well, I'm not sure I believe what it said, considering the source."

"Because it was paid for by the Grandin and Lattimore families? It's their land. How is that any different than you having oil rights and wanting them verified? They wanted to know what was on their property. Seems perfectly reasonable to me."

"They have every reason to lie."

"Well, I don't know about that, but I can tell you that Henry Lawrence, the original surveyor, would never do that. My father was a geologist and he was friends with Henry. He's incredibly well respected. One of the best in the business. If he found no oil, then there's likely no oil. He wouldn't put his name on any report that lied about what was on that property."

"If you believe so strongly in what he found, then why not say that in your survey?"

"Because I wasn't able to do the tests that he did. I can't copy someone else's work. It wouldn't be ethical."

He laughed, but there was a sharp and dismissive tone to the sound. "*Ethical*. That's a funny word to throw around when we're talking about the Grandins and the Lattimores. I don't think a single one of them is familiar with the term."

Heath was clinging to bitter doubt like it was the only thing he had going for him. She wanted to understand why. "Can I ask a question? Is this a dispute over oil rights? Or is there something else to it?"

"Very astute observation. This *is* about more than

oil. It's about two rich and powerful patriarchs trying to silence a single mom because they didn't want to take responsibility for the child one of their sons fathered. That child was my half sister, Ashley."

Bingo. So this *was* about a paternity case. The one people in Royal had been talking about. "And the single mom is your mother?"

"Was my mother. She's deceased. As is Ashley. Both of them gone too soon. Ash's birthday was last week. She would've been thirty-eight. She had so much life ahead of her."

Ruby suddenly understood what this was really about—loss and grief. Ruby had wrestled with that for more years than she liked to admit. Trying to escape the pain had brought her to Royal. Doing a quick calculation in her head, and understanding what Heath was going through, was the only reason she was about to bring up one detail she'd noticed when she'd gone over the paperwork relating to oil rights. Before, it didn't matter, but now it might give Heath some clarity. "Did you happen to look at the date on Henry's original survey?"

"I never saw it. I was only told about it. By my lawyer."

"We should confirm it, but going by Ashley's birthday, I'm pretty sure Henry's survey was done a full year before they granted rights to your mother."

Heath froze while white-hot anger rose in his face like a flash flood. "Seriously?"

Ruby swallowed hard, understanding what this meant. "Yes."

"So those bastards knew all along that it was worthless. They have piles and piles of money and they purposely looked for something of no value to give to my mother, just to shut her up." He dragged his hand through his hair, then frantically scrubbed his jaw, seeming frustrated and in some ways at war with himself. "They not only lied to her, they tricked her. Of all the low things someone could do, this might be the lowest."

"I'm sorry. I didn't want to be the bearer of bad news."

"I need to go. Now. I'm sorry I bothered you." He stormed out of the room.

For a moment, she hesitated. Did she really want to get involved with this? No. But she hated the thought of two rich and powerful families taking advantage of a struggling woman. "Heath. Wait!"

"Thank you for your help, Ruby. I'm sorry if I interrupted your day." He flung open the front door and slammed it behind him.

"Wait!" She grabbed the knob and opened it again, but she couldn't run after him with nothing more than thick wool socks on her feet. She grabbed her boots, noticing that the snow was coming down sideways and the wind had picked up significantly. There was little to no visibility. She wasn't sure how fast he was walking, but he was already nothing more than a

shadowy figure out there. He was a fool for wanting
to ride off in this. "Heath. Please stop." She worked
her feet into her boots, grabbed a coat and stomped
out onto her front porch.

He must have heard her footfalls on the wood
planks, because he turned back to her. "I've got to
be somewhere. Just let me go. Please go back in the
house." He waved her off with his hand.

"No. Don't rush off when you're angry." She
scrambled down the stairs and shuffled across her
driveway, which was now slippery in spots. The
snow was not only still coming down fast, it was
incredibly heavy. The branches of the trees surround-
ing them strained in the wind, weighed down with
the winter precipitation, swaying and bobbing like
a drunken man. "The weather is too bad. I don't
think it's a good idea to be on the ro—" A deafen-
ing crack sliced through the air. It was wood split-
ting. Ruby startled and keeled back on her heels. She
backpedaled, but there was no grip. Her feet flew
out from under her. *Thud.* Her butt hit the driveway.
Pain blinded her. It sizzled down her legs and up her
back. More cracks came, then a loud boom, followed
by the ground shaking.

Heath lunged for her, but it only made it worse.
He landed on his knee and grabbed her shoulder, but
the momentum flattened Ruby against the pavement
with Heath practically on top of her. His eyes were
even wilder and untamed this close, his lips slack

as they both struggled to catch their frosty breaths. "What the hell was that?" he asked. "It felt like an earthquake."

"The tree," she answered, trying to ignore how much she liked having his body weight against her. She gestured behind him with a nod. A bald cypress, which had to be more than sixty feet tall, had come down, landing across the road and blocking all access to her house. That thing had shown signs of deterioration a few months ago. She should have had it removed, but it was too late for that. "It fell. You aren't going anywhere."

He turned away from her and shook his head in disbelief. "This doesn't make any sense. We don't get this kind of weather in Royal."

She laughed. She couldn't help it. She could not believe Heath Thurston.

"What?" he asked, seeming indignant.

"You're arguing with what is right in front of you. Snow. A thousand-pound tree blocking your way off my property." She looked skyward and squinted as fat, icy flakes landed on her face. It was really coming down. Yes, she preferred the heat of a Texas summer to a snowstorm. But it was a change of pace, and she appreciated that. She lowered her head and settled her sights on Heath again. He was nice to look at, even when his hair was wet from snow and his cheeks ruddy and red from the cold. "A little help?" she asked.

He blinked and nodded like her words had shaken him awake. "Of course. Sorry. Are you okay?" He threaded his arm under hers, wrapping his hand around her waist and helping her to stand. He held her close once they were on their feet.

For a split second, she thought about kissing him. It would be amazing to get lost in the sheer pleasure of a kiss. But enough outlandish things had already happened in the last five minutes. She didn't need to add to the list. "I'm okay." She took a step back from him, just to break the allure of being in his strong arms. "We should get inside. I should call someone about getting that tree hauled off or we'll be stuck here forever." She was wet and cold, and one side of her ass was throbbing.

"But I really need to speak to my brother. Now." Deep creases formed in his forehead, as if he was not yet convinced that he was stuck there. He raised his cell phone in the air and peered up at the screen. "There's no phone service either."

"Guess that means no one is coming to remove that tree anytime soon."

"But I have to go."

"Is this a matter of life or death?"

"To me? It's the most important thing."

She was tired of talking in circles with this man. Handsome or not, he was going to drive her up a wall. "But will anyone die if you come back inside with me, warm up and let the weather pass?"

He grumbled quietly and tossed his head from side to side as if he was weighing his options. "No. I suppose not."

"Okay, then." She turned and started for the house, being careful not to slip and fall again.

"Okay, then, what?"

She kept going. Hopefully he had enough sense to follow her inside. "Okay, then, get back in my house before we both end up as icicles."

"Do I have to take off my boots this time?"

A breathy laugh escaped her lips as she took the first step up to the porch. She wasn't sure how long Heath Thurston was going to be at her house, but she had a feeling this was going to be a long visit. "Yes. I'm not letting you off the hook this time."

Two

Heath was frustrated, cold, and his knee was killing him. But at least he was inside with a beautiful woman.

"You can't turn me down for a drink this time. I won't let you." Ruby removed her boots, then slid him a stern sideways glance that said the other thing he'd better not refuse was removing his boots.

He planted a hand against her front door and pulled off his boots one by one. "Bourbon?"

She cocked an eyebrow. "Going straight to the hard stuff?"

"It's almost five o'clock and my knee is about to swell up to the size of a basketball." He wasn't the only one who'd been injured out in her driveway.

"I'm guessing your…you know…*backside* isn't doing much better."

"My *ass*? Oh, I'm going to end up with a nasty bruise. I'm sure of it." She enticed him closer with a wave of her hand, then turned to walk down the hall.

He followed, smiling, loving that she was not a woman who tried to hide from anything. He was also a big fan of the view as he studied the hypnotic sway of her hips. It was hard to keep from imagining what her ass looked like when it wasn't wrapped up in a pair of jeans. "Sorry about everything outside. I get a little…" *A little what? Self-possessed? Irrational?* He didn't want to think about words like that when describing himself. His actions made sense to him, and no one else had walked in his shoes. But he could imagine how outward appearances might show him in a less flattering light. "Overly determined."

"So that's what you call it."

"For now, yes."

"Got it." Ruby trailed through her cozy living room, which had tall ceilings accented by hewn wood beams and a stunner of a fireplace with a surround of hand-placed river rocks. Flames danced and flickered, casting a glow and warming up the room, which was decorated in shades of white and cream with the occasional bit of pale pink. These were feminine surroundings he wasn't quite accustomed to anymore, but when his mother and half sister were still alive, these softer touches would have felt as familiar as anything. Ruby came to a stop before the only dark piece in the entire space, an antique mahogany bar cabinet. She opened one of the doors, revealing a jaw-dropping array of bourbon bottles.

Heath had to step closer, if only to examine the many brands and ages of bourbon she had on hand. "I'm not speechless very often, but I am right now. I'm impressed. You're a serious collector. I consider myself a connoisseur, but even I don't have this extensive an assortment at home."

She looked at the bottles and quietly sighed. She even reached out and touched one with the tip of her finger. "I actually don't drink it. I'm more of a wine person. But I can't bring myself to part with these."

"You definitely should *not* part with them. If you're ever thinking of doing that, call me first. I'll happily buy the entire collection from you."

She turned to him, but only held eye contact for a moment. "It's not for sale."

Now Heath was confused—she didn't drink it, but she also didn't want to get rid of it? "Did it belong to someone special?"

"It did." She cleared her throat. "Which one would you like to try?"

Heath found himself even more confounded. Clearly, the previous owner of the bourbon was not someone she cared to discuss. Or at least not now. After all, they barely knew each other. "I'll try the

Willett. The twenty-four year. I've only had it once. It's exceptional."

"Sure thing." She took a highball glass from a shelf inside the cabinet. "Here. Pour yourself as much as you like. Can I get you any ice?"

"Absolutely not." Heath popped the cork from the bottle and slowly poured the deep amber liquid into his glass. "This is meant to be enjoyed as is." He carefully put the bottle back in place and rolled the liquor in the highball, smelling the fragrance and admiring the color. "Are you going to join me?"

"I'll have a glass of wine with dinner. For now, I'm going to go heat up the mug of cocoa I was drinking when you got here."

Heath looked out one of the windows along the back side of the house. Impossibly, the snow seemed to be coming down even harder. "I suppose I will be here at least that long, huh?" He finally took a sip of the bourbon, which was even better than he remembered.

"At least until there's cell service and I can call someone to get that tree out of my driveway." Ruby strode to the other side of the open space and rounded a butcher block peninsula, into the heart of her kitchen. She placed a ceramic coffee cup in the microwave and hit a few buttons.

"If I had a chain and a chain saw and an extra hand or two, we could slice it up and haul it out of there with my truck."

The microwave beeped and she retrieved her drink, wrapping her hands around the mug and closing her eyes to smell the steaming liquid inside. Damn, she was beautiful. She was enough to make him forget why he'd come here in the first place. Her eyes slowly opened and she took a sip, looking at him while she did it. It was a penetrating glance, one that seemed to get right down to his core. "Don't take this the wrong way, but you don't really strike me as a man who does that sort of work for himself."

For the first time in a long time, Heath found that his first reaction to that kind of probing or inquisition was not to put up his guard. It only made him more curious about her. What was going on behind those mysterious green eyes? "I own and run a sizable ranch. Now, granted, I don't do a lot of the day-to-day work. I have a whole crew working for me. But I know how to do it all. I *have* done it all, and I'm not a man who's afraid to get his hands dirty." Despite the considerable revenue and income his ranch generated, Heath still thought of himself as a working man. He hadn't come from old money like the Grandins or Lattimores had. And even though he'd inherited the ranch that eventually earned millions, it hadn't been much when he'd started. In fact, the ranch had been in such disrepair that his brother, Nolan, had wanted no part of it.

"Can you saddle a horse?" Ruby returned to the

living room and took a seat on the comfortable sofa nearest the fireplace.

Heath followed her lead and joined her, sitting at the opposite end. "Of course."

"Rope a steer?"

"It might not be pretty, but I can get it done."

"Ever birthed a calf?"

"Again, might not be pretty, but I can hold my own."

That made her smile and her eyes twinkle. "You're not quite what I expected, Heath Thurston."

"You aren't quite what I expected, either," he said. That was the understatement of the century. This whole day had come as a complete surprise. "How does a young woman become a surveyor?"

"Not easily. It's such a male-dominated field, but I can't imagine doing anything else. It was my dad's influence. He was a geologist. My mother passed away when my brother, Joe, and I were young. Dad had to travel for work all the time, all over the state of Texas, so he brought us with him." Ruby pulled her knee up onto the couch and turned to face him directly. "We were a very tight little family, and he was an amazing dad. So it was only natural that I wanted to go into something along the lines of what he did. My brother did the same. He's an environmental scientist."

"Is it hard to make a living as a surveyor?"

"It's not pretty, but I can get it done."

He laughed at the way she'd effortlessly tossed his own words back at him. She was quick, with a very appealing spark. "Like I said a few minutes ago, you definitely aren't what I expected either."

"I'm not really sure what that means, to be honest."

He cleared his throat, thinking about what had been running through his head as he'd driven up her driveway. "Your appearance. Your, uh, age."

"I'm thirty years old. Or I will be next week. Why?" Her eyes scanned his face, zipping back and forth like she was looking for clues. Or answers. "Hold on a minute. How old did you think I was?" She ended the question by reaching over and pushing on his shoulder with her fingertips. Damn, she was sexy when she confronted or questioned him, which seemed to be often.

"It doesn't matter."

"You don't want to tell me, do you?"

"Really. Let's talk about something else."

"Heath…I'm going to drag it out of you one way or another. We are stuck here for the foreseeable future. I have nothing but time on my hands right now."

He swallowed hard, fighting an urge to smile or maybe even laugh. "Fine. It's just that I pictured a much older woman. In my defense, even you said that your full name is a bit old-fashioned." He watched as a look of horror crossed her face. Heath was prepared to do anything to make it go away. "I'm not saying I don't love your name. I do. It's beautiful. Just like you."

Any offense she'd taken quickly melted away, replaced by skepticism. A woman as gorgeous and beguiling as her had surely heard hundreds of men tell her something similar. "I think the bourbon's getting to you."

"It's not." *You are. Somehow.* "Plus, the one time we talked on the phone, your voice sounded pretty rough-and-tumble."

"Like a woman who'd been through a lot?"

"Yes. Exactly."

"Well, I had a nasty cold when we talked. If my voice was scratchy, that's why."

"So you haven't been through a lot?" He didn't want to pry, but he was genuinely curious to know more, especially about whoever had once owned that bourbon collection.

"I've been through plenty." She sipped from her mug again. "But we've all been through the wringer in one way or another, haven't we?"

Heath's breath hitched in his chest as her words rang clear in his head. If only she knew how strongly that statement resonated with him. It was like having someone shine a light on his soul.

Ruby was well aware she was deflecting by saying that everyone had gone through hard times, but it was her instinct to keep her memories and her pain to herself, especially as those things related to her fiancé, Lucas. She didn't know Heath very well, and although she'd had nearly three years to process the loss of her fiancé, she liked to keep the anguish from bubbling up to the surface when she was around other people. It was easier that way. But that didn't mean she wanted to skirt all serious subject matter with Heath. She wanted to know more about what he'd been through. Everything people in Royal said about him wasn't holding true for her. He didn't seem vindictive. He seemed like a strong man hiding his vulnerability. Those two things were *not* the same.

"Do you want to tell me about your mom and sister?" she finally asked. "They're at the heart of this dispute over the oil rights, aren't they?"

Heath rolled the bourbon around in his glass, studying the liquid and drawing attention to his hands, which were admittedly amazing, a perfect marriage of strength and grace. "What do you want to know?"

Ruby was surprised he was so willing to share. She shrugged and sat back in her seat. "I'm not going anywhere and neither are you, so tell me everything."

Once again, his vision was trained on what was in his glass and not on her. She didn't know him well, but she could tell that the gears in his head were turning. She wanted desperately to know what he was thinking, making her hope just as hard that he would spill at least a few of the secrets he must be keeping tucked away in his mind.

"My dad died when my twin brother, Nolan, and I were far too young to understand the magnitude of losing him. My mom had always been a melancholy person, but after he died, the sadness she went through was profound. And it never went away. It was very hard."

"I'm sorry. I lost my mom when I was seven. I know how difficult it is to lose a parent, especially when you're too young to process it. The older you get, the farther away they are. And you question your memories of them all the time."

He nodded and looked over at her. "That's so true. All of it." He drew in a deep breath—so deep that it made his shoulders rise up near his ears. "And for me, I have so many memories of wondering if I was somehow responsible for my mother's sadness. Like it was up to me to make her happy. I don't know where I got that idea from, but it was always with me. A sense of responsibility. It was always there. Maybe I got that from my dad. From the time I could walk, I followed him, learning everything it took to keep the ranch running. Our half sister, Ashley, had to step up, practically became a mom to Nolan and me. We were always fighting her on it. We thought we were old enough to take care of ourselves, but she was five years older. She knew more than we did. Either way, we all had to grow up quickly. Our dad had run the ranch, so I took over and was determined not to fail him or my mom. Nolan tried to help for a while, but his interests were elsewhere."

Ruby was taken aback by the idea of Heath and his siblings trying to tackle such a monumental job. "How did you manage?"

"Our dad had some great ranch hands who all stayed on out of a sense of duty to our mom. I always sensed that they knew she'd been through a lot. It wasn't until recently that I figured out that her sadness went well beyond losing our dad. It was because of the way the Grandin family had treated her and Ashley."

"Ashley being half Grandin, right?"

"Yes. Her dad was Daniel Grandin. He had a fling with my mom when she was young and then took off. He lives over in France now. He claims he never knew Mom was pregnant. His father, Victor Grandin Sr., knew and wanted it kept a secret. By all accounts, my mother really struggled when Ashley was a baby. She was broke and all on her own. And then there were the Grandins, without a care in the world, sitting on their piles of money."

Ruby was starting to appreciate where Heath's bitterness came from. "How did the Lattimores get involved?"

"Those two families have been thick as thieves for generations. Augustus Lattimore and Victor John Grandin were best friends, and their properties are adjacent to each other. Now that you've told me about the date on the old survey, I believe the rotten bastards conspired to buy off my mom with the phony oil rights so she'd never tell anyone Ashley was half Grandin. They were deathly afraid my mom would talk and tarnish the Grandin name, which would have negatively impacted their family fortune, which then would have trickled down to the Lattimores. Rich people like their friends to be rich, too. They figured a worthless piece of paper was enough to shut my mother up."

"You'd think they would have worried about her claiming the rights. Eventually their lies would have caught up with them."

"I think they knew that she didn't have the strength or resources to do anything about it, so she'd never find out they tricked her."

"Augustus Lattimore is still alive, isn't he?" Ruby had heard people in town talk about him. Apparently his health was declining, but he had to be in his nineties, so that was no big surprise. "Can't someone ask him?"

Heath shook his head. "Both families clammed up as soon as I discovered the paperwork for the oil rights in my mother's effects and started looking into it. That's part of why I asked my brother, Nolan, to come back to Royal. To help me try to crack the case of those two families. But that opened up a whole new can of worms."

"In what way?"

He sighed. "Nolan had left Royal when he was eighteen. He was tired of feeling responsible for so much. But that left me here, taking care of the ranch and my mom and helping Ashley. A lot of resentment has built up between us, and it's getting better, but we've still got a ways to go. He came back to Royal to help, but then he fell in love with Chelsea Grandin, and now they're married. So of course he thinks I should drop the whole thing. But I'm not ready to do that. I still feel like I need to make things right for my mom and Ashley."

"What about Daniel Grandin? Ashley's father? Have you met him or talked to him?"

"No. The family has closed ranks and won't let me anywhere near him." He ran his hand through his hair, seeming frustrated again. "Basically, I have a whole lot of questions and not enough definitive answers. I know people see me as a bitter villain, but all I'm trying to do is get some justice for my mom and sister. I know they're gone, but it's hard for me to let it go. Sometimes I feel haunted by the whole situation. By them." His voice quaked as it trailed off. He avoided looking at Ruby, seeming embarrassed by the show of emotion.

"When did your mom and sister pass away?"

"It's been a few years now. Car accident. A truck driver ran a red light."

Ruby sucked in a sharp breath as her heart physically ached. Her biggest strength—or weakness, depending on the situation—was empathy. She had no problem putting herself in other people's shoes and feeling their pain, but everything Heath had been through hit impossibly close to home. "I am so incredibly sorry. I understand everything you're feeling." She reached out and touched his shoulder, trying to ignore the electricity that zipped through her fingertips and up her arm.

"Because of your mom?"

She hesitated for a moment, unsure if she wanted to talk about Lucas. But the pain of losing her mom was decades old. It wasn't as raw as the pain of having lost her fiancé. And she wanted Heath to know she'd struggled greatly with this, too. "My fiancé, Lucas, died. Nearly three years ago. It was an aortic aneurysm. We had no warning. It was like a light switch was turned off and he was gone."

Heath turned to the bar cabinet, then back to Ruby. "That's where the bourbon came from?"

She nodded eagerly, smiling at her good memories of Lucas. "Yes. He was the collector. Absolutely loved it. It keeps me company, even if I don't drink it."

He looked down at his glass. "And you shared it with me? We hardly know each other. I feel terrible now."

She shook her head and dared to touch him again. "Oh, no. Don't. He would want you to have it. He would have wanted someone to appreciate it."

"Are you sure?"

"I'm positive. Absolutely." Before she could say more, the lights overhead flickered. She caught a glimpse of the weather outside. "I didn't think it was possible, but it looks even worse out there. I really hope we don't lose power."

"Yeah. That would not be fun."

"Although, there's plenty of bourbon. And firewood. And I have a gas stove, so we could still eat. It wouldn't be entirely bad." *Cooped up all alone. Just the two of us.*

Their gazes connected, and for the first time, one corner of his mouth turned up in an off-kilter smile. "I know I don't know you that well, Ruby, but I have to say that you are a remarkable human being."

Heat flooded her cheeks. Her heart started pounding. She didn't deserve such praise, but it felt good. "*Remarkable* is a pretty strong word."

"It absolutely applies. You're strong. You're smart and you seem to have great intuition. And if it's not too forward of me, you're so beautiful."

It wouldn't be a stretch to kiss him. In some ways, it would be the easiest thing in the world. But also the scariest. Who was she kidding? Any guy was a leap for her, even after three years. But a man like

Heath? He was too much—too handsome, too rich and definitely too complicated. She could see her way past the first two, but that last one? If she was going to get involved with someone, she wasn't ready for serious, and she was certain that "serious" was Heath's middle name. "That's sweet of you to say, but I'm just being me. I don't know another way to be."

The lights flickered again, and they both looked up at the ceiling. A second later, the room fell into darkness. Outside, the wind howled. Inside, Ruby was painfully aware of her proximity to Heath and the way her heart was fluttering.

"I'm sure it'll come back on soon," Ruby said. "I'm on the same grid with the public works department and the animal shelter. They don't usually let them go too long without power."

Heath nodded in the direction of the fireplace. "You've already got a good amount of firewood inside, but we should grab some more, just in case the power company isn't able to get a team out here quickly. The roads can't be in good condition."

"Right. That's smart." Ruby got up from the sofa. "I'm on it."

Heath grabbed her arm. "No. I'll do it."

They both stared at the vision of his hand on her arm. She'd touched him several times in the last hour or so, but this was the first time he'd returned the favor. He didn't let go and she didn't budge an inch. Between them, there was a distinct charge in the air.

It was more than electricity. It was attraction…and sex. And for the first time in what felt like a lifetime, Ruby was seriously thinking of hopping on board.

Three

Heath trudged through the snow and battled the wind until he reached the woodpile at the side of Ruby's house. He was all for equality between the sexes, but he also believed in being a gentleman, and that meant he wasn't about to let her go outside in a blizzard for firewood. That seemed like his job.

Plus, he needed to cool off and collect his thoughts. It'd felt so good to drop his guard and tell Ruby his story. He hadn't realized how much he'd needed a sympathetic ear until he had one, and she was nothing short of that. It was hard to wrap his head around such a generous nature. After months of battling with the Grandins and the Lattimores, and having everyone in town think he was an asshole, it was a revelation to have someone simply listen and sympathize. And damn if she wasn't more gorgeous and sexy than any woman he'd been in the company of in recent history. He hadn't dated in more than a year. The only woman he'd kissed during that time was Caitlyn Lattimore, but he preferred not to think about that. She'd used him to make her boyfriend Dev jealous.

The curious thing about Ruby's brand of beauty was that the more he talked to her, the more potent it became. Her generous interior matched her pretty exterior. As far as Heath was concerned, there was too little of that in the world. Most people cared about superfluous things like money and power. Appearances. That was what had driven the Grandin and Lattimore families to deceive his mother and deny his sister her birthright. Heath cared about right and wrong. And Ruby seemed to be cut from the same cloth.

He finished stacking firewood in the canvas log tote Ruby had given to him, loading it up until there was simply no more room. There was no telling how long the power would be out and he didn't want either of them to be cold. Granted, there was a fair amount of heat between him and Ruby—at least, as far as he was reading it. But he was so far out of practice when it came to sex and romance, mostly because he'd shut himself off from the world when his mom and Ashley died. Grief did that to a person.

He made his way back around to the front door,

following the path he'd made on his way to the wood-pile. He was quick to close the front door when he stepped inside, not wanting to let out any trapped heat. Immediately he noticed a faint glow coming from the living room and kitchen that hadn't been there before. He worked his way out of his jacket and tugged off his boots, then toted the firewood down the hall. When he stepped into the great room, Ruby was busy in the kitchen.

"How was it out there?" she asked with her back to him as she used a flashlight to check the contents of a kitchen cabinet. She'd lit candles, which were everywhere. It was romantic. Dangerously so.

"Cold. And windy. It's a whole lot nicer in here." That was an understatement. Ruby's cottage was a cozy retreat. It might be small and quaint, but it felt like a real home. He carried the firewood to the hearth and first grabbed some of the older, dry logs from a metal rack and carefully placed them atop the fire. Then he unloaded the cold, wet wood he'd brought in from outside so it could dry out.

"Thanks for braving the storm. I appreciate it. I raided the fridge while you were gone. I had some homemade pasta sauce in the freezer, so I'm heating that up now. It won't be fancy, but you'll at least get a hot meal."

"Sounds amazing to me." Heath poked at the fire as the logs began to smolder and catch flame. He shut the screen, then walked over to the kitchen.

She turned and smiled at him. Had she somehow managed to get prettier while he was outside? "Red wine okay? I've got a cabernet and a merlot."

"Cabernet, if that's all right with you."

"Nice. You like something with a little more body?" She pulled out a corkscrew and began opening the bottle.

"I suppose I do." Heath cleared his throat, trying to keep from thinking about Ruby's body and how spectacular it was. Her gentle curves were exactly his speed, and if he spent too much time imagining what she looked like from head to toe, he might be tempted to do something rash, like ask if he could convince her to part with some of her clothes. "Is there anything I can do to help?"

"You can grab some glasses. Top shelf of the cabinet next to the fridge."

Heath rounded the kitchen peninsula and pulled out two stemmed wineglasses, then turned and placed them on the counter. This was the closest they'd stood to each other, aside from that moment in the driveway when he'd had her in his arms. He liked being near her. She smelled amazing, the softest floral fragrance he'd ever breathed in. Her hair tumbled over her shoulders in soft waves, begging to be touched. Her eyes were so full of sincerity and honesty that they simply took his breath away. He was drawn to Ruby in a way he couldn't explain. He felt like a lonely planet being pulled into a new orbit, one that left him revolving around Ruby like she was the sun. Between the weather and being with her, it felt as if he'd arrived in a whole new world.

She poured the wine and handed him his glass, then lifted hers to toast. "To being inside. Because I sure as hell wouldn't want to be outside right now."

He grinned and clinked his glass with hers. "As the person who went to get the firewood, I'm in complete agreement." As he drew in a slow sip of his wine, he found himself overcome by the most unfamiliar feeling—optimism. He not only hadn't felt that way in quite some time, he wasn't sure what exactly it was that he had to feel optimistic about. On paper, his life was a mess. He spent his days trying to find justice for his sister and mother, and his nights all alone and wondering how he could continue this battle as a one-man army. His brother, Nolan, was certainly of little help. For now, he only knew that he was looking forward to spending the night in this cottage in the woods. With her.

"Will your animals be okay out on the ranch?"

Thankfully, he and the few ranch hands working the week between Christmas and New Year's had taken care of it earlier that day, at the first sign of bad weather. "Yes. They're all tucked away in their respective barns and stables. I had solar panels installed a few years ago, so even the power outage won't impact the heaters that kick in when it gets cold."

"That's good to hear." Ruby turned to look at the stove. "Oh. Water's boiling. Time for pasta."

"You do that. I'll go give the fire another poke." He took his wine and headed for the fireplace, wondering how tonight was going to play out. Dinner was a given. They'd finish that bottle of wine. Then what? He was clearly staying over, but if the power didn't come back on, the smart thing would be for the two of them to sleep as close to the fire as possible. And if they were really smart, they'd cozy up next to each other. But as for how he was going to bring that up, he did not know. He crouched in front of the hearth and poked at the fire as it warmed his face and kept his mind racing. If anyone had told him that morning that his trip to visit Ruby would turn into this, he never would have believed them.

"Pasta will be ready in a few minutes," Ruby said, startling him. She'd walked into the living room so quietly that he hadn't even noticed. "I'd love to eat at the table like grown-ups, but I think it's best if we stay close to the fire as much as possible. Even with the stove on, it's starting to get a little chilly in the kitchen. So let's eat right here, if that's okay with you." She set her wineglass down on the floor near the hearth.

He turned and looked up at her as he remained crouched in front of the fire. "I'm not formal or fancy, Ruby. I'm happy to eat wherever you think we should."

"Okay. Great." She started for the kitchen again, then turned back to him. "Are you coming? I'm going to need help."

Heath straightened and followed her. "What can I do?"

"There's a tablecloth in the top drawer of the buffet near the bar cabinet. Grab that and spread it out on the floor in front of the fireplace. We'll have a picnic." She pulled a pair of pretty cloth napkins and some silverware out of the drawer. "And then you can set these out. And maybe see if there are more candles in the buffet?"

"Got it." Heath did exactly as she asked, soon finding himself rummaging through the contents of the vintage cabinet. The tablecloth was easy enough to find, but the candles were proving more difficult. In the bottom drawer, he came across something that stopped him dead in his tracks. A thick notebook labeled "Wedding Plans." It had been one thing to hear about her fiancé passing away, but it was quite another to be confronted by evidence of their relationship and the future she'd once thought she'd have with him. He closed the drawer quickly. "I don't see any more candles."

"Okay. I think I have more in the front closet. We can look after dinner."

He turned to see her standing in the living room, holding two bowls of steaming pasta. "Sorry." He rushed over, and with a snap, he shook out the tablecloth and allowed it to settle on the floor before the fire. She handed him his bowl and they both took a seat. "This smells absolutely amazing."

"Thanks. I hope you like it." She took her glass in hand, then raised it for another toast. "To surprises."

Heath reached up to take his glass from the end table where he'd placed it earlier. He looked deeply into her eyes and he toasted her in return, wondering what exactly he'd done to deserve an opportunity to spend time with such a gorgeous woman. "Absolutely. To surprises."

"Speaking of surprises, I never imagined we'd sleep together on the first date, but I don't see how it makes any sense to do anything but that." She twirled the noodles on her fork and popped the bite into her mouth.

Heath froze. "Uh…"

She swallowed her food, then reached out and knocked his shoulder with the back of her hand. "Oh, my God. You can wipe that look of horror off your face, Heath. I'm just giving you a hard time again. I was only trying to say that we're going to have to sleep in here tonight. And if we're smart, we'll keep each other warm."

He exhaled, feeling grateful that she'd taken the time to clarify what she meant. They were on the same page. It was definitely the smartest solution to their predicament, aside from keeping the fire stoked. But exactly how much of a trial would it be to keep this a platonic arrangement? "I was thinking the same thing earlier. I just wasn't quite sure how to bring it up. I didn't want you to think I'm not a gentleman. Or that I was trying to take advantage of the situation."

"I realize we don't know each other very well, but you seem like the perfect gentleman to me."

He laughed quietly. "There are a few dozen people in this town who would like to disagree with you."

"Maybe they just don't know you. Or understand where you're coming from."

"Or maybe they simply care about their own interests more than they care about right or wrong."

She took a long sip of her wine, not taking her eyes off him. "Nothing you can do or say will convince me that you aren't a perfect gentleman."

Well, that certainly took all sexy thoughts he'd had earlier off the table. But maybe that was for the best. After seeing that notebook in the bottom of Ruby's buffet, Heath was starting to think that, as much as he wanted Ruby, it might not be a good idea to get involved with a woman who was living with what was likely a very fragile heart. Instead, he might just need to devote himself to protecting it.

Ruby was at war with herself after she'd made that boneheaded comment about sleeping together on the first date. Why did she have to turn things into a joke? Probably because it was her defense mechanism. Humor was a great way to deflect, and she was a champion at it.

But still, sleeping close was a practical solution to their predicament, right? It was the sensible thing to do. Then why did it make Ruby so nervous? Why did it make her feel so self-conscious to have suggested it? *You just told a sexy and handsome man who you hardly know that you think it's a good idea to sleep in the same bed as him. That was a bold move, Ruby Rose Bennett. Incredibly bold.*

They ate in near silence, nothing but the quiet crackle and pop of the fire to fill the void between them.

Heath finished eating first. "That was delicious. Thank you."

"You're so welcome." Ruby set aside her bowl, leaving the few remaining bites. She was too filled with nervousness to eat any more. She decided she was not going to circle back to the subject of keeping each other warm that night, so she asked about anything else she could think of, like his ranch and growing up in Royal. Heath reciprocated, inquiring about her career. They steered clear of more serious topics, like the death of his mom and sister, or Ruby's own loss, of her fiancé. She marveled at how easy it was to talk to Heath. He might be stubborn and a bit single-minded, but at his core, he seemed kind and thoughtful.

"It's getting late. We should probably revisit the

question of sleeping arrangements," Heath said several hours later.

"Right. We don't have to do what I suggested earlier. Unless you're okay with it." She swallowed hard, daring to look into his eyes, even when a single glance made it feel like he was hypnotizing her.

"I think it only makes sense. We have to sleep and we have to stay warm. That's the smartest idea."

Her stomach flipped at the thought of being that close to him. "Great. Good. I was thinking we could drag my mattress in here and put it in front of the fire. That'll be more comfortable than the floor."

"Sounds good. No time like the present." Heath got up, then reached for her to help her stand.

She was perfectly capable of getting up on her own, but she wasn't about to protest. Instead, she put her hand in his, relishing this bit of male attention. It felt so good, like she was her old self. That person she'd been three or four years ago. "My bedroom is just down the hall."

Heath followed Ruby to her room.

"I guess we'll grab the bedding and pillows, and then we'll carry the mattress into the living room. I've got a bunch of extra blankets we can use, too," she said.

"The hall is pretty narrow. Let me take the mattress. You can take the smaller things."

"You sure?"

"Positive."

There it was again—Heath and his gentlemanly ways. She admired that he was like that.

He walked around to the other side of the bed and playfully tossed a pillow in her direction, smiling.

Ruby entertained a fleeting thought—crashing into him and kissing him and pulling him down on top of her right here and now. They could make their own fire. Together. In this bed. "Sounds like a plan."

They followed Heath's suggestion, and a few short minutes later, he had the mattress perfectly situated on the floor in front of the fire, right where they'd eaten. Ruby handed him one end of a clean fitted sheet, then dropped down to her knees to put it on.

Heath followed suit, but he recoiled the instant he reached the floor. "Oh. Ow." He popped back and landed on his butt next to the bed. "That wasn't very smart of me. I forgot about my knee."

"Would you like me to get some ice?" Ruby crawled across the mattress to where he was sitting.

"I'm okay. Really. It's just a little tender. How's your butt doing?"

She grinned. "Are you flirting with me?"

He looked at her and their gazes connected. "Of course. You're so beautiful it'd be stupid for me not to."

Her heart pounded frantically. She was painfully aware of every breath. "So, you're not flirting. You're kidding."

"I'm not. It's the truth."

She bit down on her lip, hard, if only to keep herself in the moment. "You're not half bad yourself."

"Now who's the flirt?"

She shrugged. "I learned from the best."

"Me? Am I the best?"

"Believe it or not, you are." It felt as though she was perched on the edge of a cliff and something was telling her to jump. In truth, all she wanted was a kiss. It had been so long since she'd kissed a man. Since she'd been able to get lost in someone. But was she ready for that? Logic said that three years was more than enough time. But that was the funny thing about loss—logic didn't matter. It was all up to the heart. And right now, her heart and body wanted Heath.

She leaned closer, closing her eyes halfway. She wanted to see the moment when he decided to give in, but she was also scared. Despite his flirting, she still felt so unsure of herself. Mercifully, one corner of Heath's lips quirked up into a smile, and she felt as though she had the green light to go for it. So she did, grasping his shoulder and pressing her mouth to his. There was no hesitation from him, only warmth and strength, exactly what she wanted from a man. When his lips parted and his tongue met hers, heat prickled across her skin, so swiftly that it made her dizzy. Her heart made a happy flip and she used her other hand to pull him closer, until his chest was pressed against hers. His fingers threaded into her hair and he gathered it at her nape, gently tugging on it and causing her to moan with pleasure. She responded by deepening the kiss, their tongues winding in an endless circle, effortlessly. He shifted to his knees, a sure sign that he didn't care at all about discomfort. She pushed her hips to meet his, relishing the moment when he got harder.

He eased them down onto their sides. She slept on this mattress every night, but it had never felt so luxurious, even though it was now supported by nothing more than the hardwood floor. Heath was all firm muscle and a capable grasp, and he rolled to his back, with Ruby on top of him. She really liked weighing him down. She liked the power of it. She liked knowing that this man who aroused so much fear and suspicion in the people of Royal wanted to be under her control.

She pressed harder against him, stomach, chest and lips. His fingers combed up through her hair, and he cupped the back of her head. His hand encouraged an even deeper kiss and the erasing of all space between them. She spread her legs wider, her knees slipping to the mattress so she was straddling his hips. She rocked into him and he groaned fiercely, slipping his warm hands up the back of her sweater and sending a brilliant and shiny thrill through her. This was not only escalating quickly, it was barreling toward somewhere she'd thought it might not go. She wanted him so badly that the need burned inside her, even hotter than the fire so nearby. Heath might end up making her spontaneously combust.

She sat up, looking down at him, marveling at how handsome he was. "I want to see you, Heath." She slipped her fingers beneath his sweater as he raised his arms to let her push the garment past his head. Inch by inch, his incredible chest and shoulders were revealed. She spread her hands across his stomach, feeling the muscles twitch beneath her touch. Every inch of him was hard, chiseled and perfection. But then she remembered how soft his lips were, so she dropped down to seek his kiss again, just to see if it was as heavenly as she remembered.

"This really isn't fair." He broke the kiss and whispered into her hair with a hot huff of breath. "You saw me. I haven't seen any of you. And it's killing me."

Ruby gnawed on her lower lip, filled with this implausible mix of desire and defensiveness. No man had seen her in recent history. Was she ready for this? She wasn't sure, but she'd come this far and she wasn't ready to stop. Not yet. She sat back and Heath followed. Then they shifted until he was leaning against the couch and her legs were wrapped around his waist. His hands curled under the hem of her sweater as she drew in a sharp breath, knowing what was coming…knowing how vulnerable she was about to be. He raised it slowly, lifting the fabric up and away, leaving her exposed to him. She was thankful for the soft glow of the fire. It made him look so amazing. He gently tossed her sweater aside, and then he reached around to the center of her back. He kissed the top of her breast, blazing a trail along the edge of her bra cup as he unhooked the clasp, then dragged the straps down her shoulders. They entered a new level of familiarity as he cast aside the bra and her breasts were left naked.

Their gazes connected as he lightly teased her nipple with his fingertips, rubbing up and down. The skin drew impossibly hard and tight, making her breasts feel warm and full and sending her body temperature spiking. He gripped her rib cage with one hand, pushing her breast higher with his fingers. Then he leaned down and drew her nipple into his warm mouth. She wanted so badly to watch him touch her like that, but it felt so impossibly good that her eyes automatically clamped shut. She rocked her center against his crotch, relishing the unbelievable tension between them. She wanted him. So badly it hurt.

"Do you have a condom?" she asked.

"I don't."

All the air seemed to escape the room. Just like that, her dream of letting go with a man disappeared and reality came back into sharper focus. "Oh."

"I'm, uh, sorry. I...I..." he stammered. "I don't exactly walk around with condoms in my pocket. I thought we were going to have a business meeting."

Ruby wondered what in the hell she'd been thinking. This was Heath Thurston. He was practically her boss. And being with him was like playing with fire. Yes, he was sexy, but if she wasn't careful, all that heat could get out of control and she'd be burned. "Right. Of course. That makes perfect sense. I don't know what I was thinking."

"It was a perfectly suitable question."

"I feel like I started something with that kiss and now it can't happen."

Heath shook his head. "Look. We were having fun and now it's time to be responsible about it."

She reached down for her sweater and clutched it to her chest. She had a deep need to cover herself. Possibly to disappear. She was embarrassed by the way she'd been so forward with him, and then by the way she'd stomped on the brakes. "I shouldn't have kissed you first. I'm not sure I was really ready for this anyway." It was miserable to admit the truth, but she couldn't be anything less than honest.

He reached over and picked up his own sweater, which Ruby took as her cue to climb off his lap. "It's okay, Ruby. Really."

She let out a frustrated sigh and grabbed her bra to put it on. "And now I feel even worse because you're stuck here for the night. And there's no heat." With every passing word, she felt her frustration grow. What a mess. And it was all of her making. She threaded her arms through her sweater and pulled it over her head. "You're just so damn handsome and nice. I'm sorry there's nowhere for you to go to get away from me."

He grinned and sat back, leaning against the sofa and shaking his head. "Ruby. I have had more fun tonight than I've had in the last several years. Please don't apologize. Let's just finish that bottle of wine, climb under the covers and say good-night."

Four

Heath woke to the sound of a chain saw and the feel of Ruby in his arms. He remained impossibly still, waiting to see if the noise outside would wake her while desperately hoping this moment wouldn't end. He closed his eyes, inhaling her smell, wishing the world away so he could have a little more time. He didn't need much. Hell, he hadn't realized he'd needed any time away from the stresses of his life at all, but now that he'd had a taste of setting aside bitter betrayal for something completely different, he wasn't ready for it to end. They'd had a magnificent night, even without sex. Still, he didn't know what to expect now that it was the morning after.

The power had come back on at some point—

the house was warmer and what was left of the fire wasn't throwing off enough heat to have accomplished that feat. Judging by what he heard coming from outside, someone was clearing the tree that was blocking the road up to Ruby's cottage. Less than twenty-four hours ago, he would have been incredibly grateful for that. It would have allowed him to race off in his truck and hunt down his brother, all so he could resume his fight against the Grandins and the Lattimores.

Ruby stirred. "It's warm in here," she muttered into his chest.

"It is. Power came back on, but we both slept right through it."

"So, technically, we don't *need* each other's body heat."

A ribbon of doubt worked its way through Heath. He felt like he'd been caught red-handed. They no longer had the pretense of needing each other for survival. "No. We don't. You're right." He let go of her and distanced himself.

She raised her head and looked him in the eye. One glance and it was like she could see right through him. "I'm just giving you crap, Heath. I liked being in your arms. It was nice."

A wide smile bloomed on his face as relief washed over him, followed quickly by a wave of raw attraction. He didn't act on it, though. He was fully committed to following her lead. "I thought so, too."

From outside came the sound of a truck beeping as it backed up. "I wonder if that's Sam out there, hauling off the tree."

"Sam?" Heath wondered for a moment if he had competition for Ruby's attention.

"He works for public works. He checks on me every now and then. I think he might have a crush on me."

A crush. Heath didn't have to wonder if he had a crush on Ruby. It was full-on infatuation and he'd spent less than a day with her. This realization didn't scare him. It brought him the first blips of happiness he'd experienced in months. Possibly years. But he sure as hell wasn't going to go around sharing that information. "Do you want me to go check?"

"I should go. It's my house. And if it is Sam, he's going to want to talk to me anyway."

"I'll come with you."

Ruby sat up and pulled on some socks over the ones she was already wearing. Her hair was a sexy mess and Heath took some pride in knowing he'd contributed to that, if only for a few minutes. He rolled off the mattress and ducked down the hall to use the bathroom while Ruby put on her boots and jacket. By the time he was done, Ruby was already out on the porch, so Heath grabbed his coat and joined her. It was a brisk morning, but the sun was bright and the snow on the tree branches was already starting to melt. Sure enough, two men were tossing chunks of that big tree into the bed of a pickup that said Royal Public Works on the side.

"There's Sam," Ruby said, pointing to the taller of the two men. "I'll be right back."

"I'll be here. I'm going to check if there's cell service. Might call my brother if there is." He watched Ruby approach the two men as he pulled his phone out of his pocket. Sure enough, the bars had returned. He dialed Nolan's number.

His brother answered after only a few rings. "How about this weather, huh?"

"Is this not the weirdest thing ever? So much snow in Royal? I can't think of another time that it was this bad."

"We would have loved this when we were kids. I felt like we always wished for snow at Christmas and we never got it."

Heath wasn't able to look back fondly at all of his childhood, but he did have a few amazing memories of Nolan from when they were younger. Being a twin was a singular experience—everyone assumed he and Nolan were impossibly close, but they'd always wanted different things. The times they found something they agreed on, those were the times Heath cherished. Nolan had gotten sick of Royal and the responsibility of the ranch, left right after high school and stayed away for most of fifteen years. So much for the solidarity of being a twin. "Hey," Heath said, "I need to talk to you about something."

"Uh-oh. Your voice just got significantly more serious. Is this about the oil rights? I told you that I'm staying out of it. I helped you when you first found the paperwork, but that's all behind me now. My relationship with Chelsea is my first priority. You know I can't get involved. You need to move on, Heath. I've told you that one hundred times."

Move on. A day ago, Heath would have thought that was impossible. Hell, even as recently as the conclusion of that first conversation with Ruby, he was ready to redouble his efforts and wage full-on war against the Grandins and Lattimores. But standing out here on this crystal clear morning, looking at Ruby, with her messy blond hair and a laugh that rivaled anything the birds in the trees were singing, he had this glimmer in his head and his heart—a very vague feeling that his life could be better. "It's just that I had a meeting with Ruby Bennett, the surveyor, yesterday."

"A meeting on a Saturday? Two days after Christmas?"

Funny, but that was the same thing Ruby had said to him. He supposed he had been pretty irrational with his timing. "I know. I got a little carried away. But she pointed out something very damning. Something that says that the Grandins knew—"

"Stop right there. Please don't say another word."

"I'm trying to tell you something. Something that is not insignificant. Something major."

"And I told you, Heath, that I want to be closer to you. I want to keep rebuilding our relationship. But I can't do that if you're going to hold on to this grudge. The only way for me to have a happy marriage with Chelsea *and* be close to you is for this entire thing to go away. You hold the key to that."

Heath grumbled under his breath, but then Ruby turned, waved at him and smiled. He felt like his insides were turning to pudding. "It's more than a grudge, Nolan. It's about right and wrong. We're talking about our mother. And our sister. Where would you and I be right now if Ashley hadn't stepped in after Dad's death? If she hadn't cared for us? Mom sure as hell wasn't capable of much. And I think we both know who's responsible for that."

"I realize all of that, Heath. And there's no question that it's sad and unfortunate. But as for the rest of it, there are no real answers because it's all in the past. Ashley and Mom knew that we loved them. And we know that they loved us. We all did our best during that time. That's got to be the end of it."

"The end?" The thought of that made something in Heath's heart twist into a tight knot. "So you want me to walk away right now? Call our lawyer and tell him we're done? It's over?"

"He's your lawyer, not mine. But if it were up to me, yes, that's what I would do."

"I've got a few more days to make that decision." Heath's lawyer, Albert Cortez, an old family friend, had asked for an update on their working relationship. If Heath no longer required his services, Albert preferred to know that before the end of the year. It made things easier from an accounting standpoint. But Albert apparently hadn't made the connection between the dates on the original oil survey and the deed to the oil rights given to Heath and Nolan's mom. That was going to require a conversation.

"Look, if you want to talk about finding ways to fund Ashley's foundation, I'm all ears," Nolan said. "But if it's going to be anything else pertaining to oil, I don't want to hear it. I love you, but I will not hesitate to hang up on you."

Maybe his brother was right. Maybe he needed to find a way to look ahead. Ruby sure made him want to. "Okay. Can we talk about the foundation, then?"

"We can definitely talk about it. Not now, though. Chelsea and I are about to go for a walk in the snow."

"Well…when, then? Don't put me off on this."

"And don't get surly with me. Chelsea and I are newlyweds. We're entitled to spend time together, especially over the holidays."

Heath felt like a heel. This was another example of him getting too wrapped up in his own head. "I'm sorry. You're right."

"It's okay. I understand. Maybe we can get together. What are you doing for New Year's Eve?"

"Nothing."

Nolan laughed. "Why does that not surprise me?"

"I never do anything on New Year's. I don't see the point. So we flip the calendar? It's just another day to me."

Nolan let out a dismissive tut. "Chelsea and I are going to the party at the Cattleman's Club. I think you should join us. There will be music and dancing and amazing food. And I think you should bring a date. It'd be good for you to have some female companionship, Heath. I worry about you all alone in that big house, working harder than any person needs to and stewing in your own juices about Mom and Ashley."

"I don't know. I'm not big on parties." And frankly, going to the Texas Cattleman's Club was a minefield in waiting. He'd been a member forever, but there was a good-sized chunk of the membership that was not a fan of his at the moment. Many people had sided with the Grandin and Lattimore families in the dispute.

"Then do it for me. I want you and Chelsea to spend more time together. My twin brother and my wife should know each other better. We didn't even get to see you at Christmas."

"I know." On paper, he welcomed the idea of being closer to Nolan and finally returning to a true family dynamic after so many years of being apart. But what was Heath supposed to talk about with Chelsea? He sure as hell couldn't ask how her family was doing.

"Then come to the party. Do you have someone you can ask?"

Heath cleared his throat. "I have an idea of someone. Yes."

"Who is it?"

"A woman. A woman I know. Or actually, a woman I know who I just met for the first time in person."

"You're talking in circles. She must be something."

Heath couldn't keep his eyes off Ruby. She was laughing as she talked to the two men, who were clearly enthralled with her. That came as no surprise. She was mesmerizing. "You could say that."

"Who is she?"

"I told you a few minutes ago. Ruby Rose Bennett."

"The surveyor? You want to bring a surveyor to a New Year's Eve party?"

"Hey. What's that supposed to mean?"

"Nothing. I'm just not really envisioning someone who wants to put on a cocktail dress and drink champagne."

Heath had no earthly idea what Ruby might wear. He'd only seen her in jeans and a sweater, but he was a huge fan of what he saw. He'd also seen a little bit more, and he would have been lying if he said he didn't want to see all of her. "For the record, she's stunning."

At the end of the driveway, one of the men closed up the back of the truck while the other climbed into the driver's seat and started the engine. The warm exhaust billowed in clouds from the tailpipe. That loud *beep beep beep* sounded as he backed up the vehicle to turn it around.

"Where are you? It sounds like a garbage truck."

"I'm at Ruby's. A tree fell across her driveway from the storm. The public works guys are here to haul it away."

"Hold on a minute. What time did you meet with her? And where?"

Dammit. Heath shouldn't have divulged where he was. His brother was going to give him a hard time about this. "I came over around four or five yesterday."

"Exactly when the storm started to get bad."

"Yes, Nolan. So what?"

"How did you get home? The roads were horrible. And then you went back this morning?"

"I stayed here. What's your point?"

Nolan laughed. "Well, I'll be damned. Now you really have to come on New Year's Eve. I want to meet Ruby the surveyor. And I won't take no for an answer."

Ruby was making her way back up to the house now that the truck was slowly heading back down her driveway.

"Fine. We'll come. I have to go. I'll talk to you later."

"I'll text you the details."

"Yeah. Sure." Heath was desperate to end the call

so he could talk to Ruby. As to how he was going to broach the subject of New Year's Eve with her, he wasn't sure.

"I hope you know how happy this makes me," Nolan added.

"Goodbye, Nolan." Heath ended the call and stuffed his phone back into his pocket. "Hey," he said to Ruby as she climbed the stairs. "All taken care of?"

"Yes. Sam is such a sweetheart. He was worried about me because he knew that the power had gone out. He drove up to check and that's when he saw the tree. He went back to get help and, well, that's how you ended up with a clear passage to civilization."

Heath then realized that, aside from the folks he paid to take care of his ranch, absolutely no one would check on him or his welfare. Not even Nolan would. He'd be too busy worrying and thinking about Chelsea. That was the difference between Ruby and him. She was kind and people clearly adored her. He was a monster who people despised. "That's really nice."

"So, yeah." Ruby looked down at the porch floor. "You're free to go whenever."

Heath wanted to take Ruby's hand, but he wasn't sure that was what she wanted, so he didn't. "I need to ask you something, but let's go back inside, okay?"

"Sure." Ruby followed him back into the house and closed the door. "Were you able to talk to your brother?"

"I was."

"What did he say about that little detail I pointed out about the old survey?"

"I didn't get that far. He didn't want to hear about it."

She nodded. "Because he's married to a member of the Grandin family."

"Right. And he said I was living in the past. He also pointed out that I can't really fix what happened because my mom and Ashley aren't here."

She drew in a deep breath through her nose. "What did you say?"

He shrugged. "There wasn't much I could say. He told me he was going to hang up if I kept talking about it."

"Okay, well, then how do you feel about it?"

Heath wasn't particularly good at talking about his feelings. Emotions were too abstract. Too unpredictable and entirely impossible to control. But Ruby made him want to try, even if he was fairly certain he wouldn't do well. "It makes me mad. He's shutting me down without listening."

"Sounds like you need to say that to him, then."

"Maybe. We'll see."

"It doesn't make him wrong. There is probably some truth to what he's telling you about not living in the past and letting things go." She reached for his arm and stepped closer. "But I also understand why you're struggling with that. Between my mom and Lucas, I've been through a lot of loss. I know what it's like to feel like the past is holding you back, but you don't know how to do anything other than cling to it because it hurt so much to lose everything you did."

It took Heath a minute to wrap his head around that. She was right. Of course. And she understood what he was going through, which helped him digest her words a bit better. But was he really clinging to the past? Or was it just that somebody, somewhere, had to right this wrong? Simply so a bit of order could be restored and he could finally sleep? And if that was the case, he was clearly the only person who could do the job. No one else had the mettle to continue with the charge. No one else cared as much as he did. "It feels good to know that you understand. It helps."

Ruby leaned against the wall and smiled softly. "Good. I'm glad. Hopefully that will help you move forward."

"I do want to figure out how to fund my sister's foundation. Maybe I need to focus on that."

"That sounds like a great idea. Having a project is good. What kind of foundation was it?"

"She wanted to open a horseback riding center for kids and adults with cognitive and physical impairments. Horseback riding can be incredibly therapeutic. Ashley learned about it when she was a teaching assistant in a classroom for autistic children. She saw what it did for their development, both physical and mental. And the kids tended to form very special bonds with the horses. It's an all-around wonderful thing."

Ruby grinned even wider now. "That sounds so amazing. I would love to help. If you're going to need volunteers or anything like that."

"Really?"

"Of course."

Up until that moment, Heath hadn't considered that anyone might help with this, aside from Nolan chipping in some money and possibly some volunteer time. "That would be so great. It was just an idea when Ashley was still alive, but I'd like to make it happen. I'm thinking I can house it on my property, and I've got money set aside to build the infrastructure, but there will be staff and ongoing maintenance, which could end up being sizable. If I can fund an endowment, it could run on its own forever and no one would ever have to pay a penny for the services. That would be the ultimate goal."

Ruby stepped closer and took his hand. It brought him immense relief to have that physical contact with her, to know that she wanted it, too. "You're a good man, Heath. A really, really good man."

He saw a tear roll down her cheek. He couldn't help but reach out and wipe it away with the back of his hand. "Do you have any idea how long it's been since someone said that to me?"

She shook her head and pressed her lips together tightly as if she was fighting back more tears. "I don't. But if it's been a while, I'm glad that I had the chance to say it."

As physically frustrated as he'd been last night that he and Ruby hadn't had sex, he was thankful for it now. There was something growing between them, and if he'd had to chalk it up to lust, he might doubt how real it was. "I need to ask you a question."

"Sure. Anything."

"Do you have plans for New Year's Eve?"

"I don't. I usually don't do anything other than put on my pj's, pop some popcorn and watch a movie."

That sounded like sheer heaven to Heath, but he did want to forge that stronger bond with Nolan. It felt like an essential on his to-do list. "My brother wants me to go to the party at the Texas Cattleman's Club. It's not really my speed, but I need to spend more time with him and my sister-in-law. I was hoping that you might come with me."

She grinned and the tears evaporated, making way for the shine of her incredibly bright eyes. "I would love to go. I've never been to the TCC. I've heard it's amazing."

"It can be fun. It can also be a runaway train if you're the subject of town gossip. But I'm going to hope for the best, and honestly, I think I can endure anything if you're with me."

"Perfect, then. I guess it's a date?"

He placed a hand at her waist, still unsure of what degree of physical contact was okay with her. He didn't want to cross any lines. "It absolutely is."

She leaned closer. "I'm sorry about last night. I'm sorry that I wasn't ready."

He shook his head. "Don't apologize. I'm happy to take things slow."

She placed a finger on his shoulder, then drew it down his chest. "I don't need things to go too slow. I just needed some time to wrap my head around it. That's all. I didn't expect a sexy man to show up on my doorstep yesterday."

Heath couldn't hide the wide grin that spread across his face. "That's going to go straight to my head, you know."

She leaned in closer, flattening her other hand against his chest. "I hope that's exactly where it will go." Her lips met his in the softest kiss he'd ever experienced. It was sweet and sexy and exactly what he needed. Everything he wanted.

And everything he hadn't taken the time to dream of.

Five

Ruby had nothing to wear to a New Year's Eve party in Royal, especially not one at the Texas Cattleman's Club. Although she'd never been, she'd heard plenty of stories. The TCC had a reputation. It was where the wealthy and powerful players of Royal gathered to make deals, hammer out problems and celebrate, usually on a very large and lavish scale. There was no way she was going to attend what had to be one of the biggest parties of the year at the club without looking spectacular. Even more to the point, she wasn't going to be Heath Thurston's date without looking perfectly put together. And sexy. If she still had it in her.

The day after the tree had been removed from her

driveway and Heath had left her by herself, the snow
in Royal was mostly melted and the roads were clear.
She hopped in her SUV and headed for the heart of
downtown to go shopping at the Rancher's Daughter. She owned plenty of cute, feminine clothes—fun
summer dresses, flirtatious skirts and formfitting
tops—but she'd worn almost none of it since Lucas
had died. It had felt unnecessary to present herself to
the world in a way that suggested she was a woman
who desired any attention or felt free. After all, Ruby
had felt neither of those things when she'd suddenly
found herself all alone. But Heath had awoken something in her, a part of her that she'd feared might
never come to life. It was time to dress herself up
and remind herself that it was okay to move on. It
might not be easy, but it was okay.

A chime sounded when Ruby opened the door to
the boutique, which was full of some of the cutest
and most stylish clothes Ruby had ever seen, all of
it artfully displayed. If money wasn't always a bit
tight, she could see herself going on a real shopping
spree here. As she slowly strolled past the racks and
shelves, she was drawn to so much, it was hard to
know where to start, except that she knew she hadn't
yet seen anything dressy enough for New Year's Eve.

A woman with fair skin and striking red hair
stepped out of the back room, talking on a cell phone.
She made eye contact with Ruby and held up a finger. "Hey, Zanai, I need to call you back. I have a

customer," she said into the phone. "Okay. 'Bye." She pressed a button on the screen and placed the device on the counter near the register. "I'm so sorry. It's my best friend. We start talking and I swear it could go all day long."

Ruby smiled, thinking that she needed more friends. She'd essentially locked herself away in her cottage since Lucas had died, refinishing floors and taking down walls. If she wasn't doing that, she was working. She had almost no social life. That had to change. "Oh, don't worry about it. I was just taking it all in. It's such a beautiful store."

"Well, aren't you sweet? I'm Morgan Grandin. This is my shop. What can I help you with today?"

Ruby froze for a moment. *Morgan Grandin.* If she had the family members straight, Morgan was the youngest of the Grandin siblings. "It's nice to meet you, Morgan. I've actually been out on your family's property. I'm a surveyor." Ruby saw no reason to hide from this fact. In her experience, it was best to be open and honest with people. It could pay big dividends.

Morgan's eyes went wide as she seemed to make the connection. "Oh, okay." She nodded eagerly and wagged her finger. "I heard about you. I think you met my older brother, Vic, when you were out there. He was out on his horse and saw you."

"Yes. I was finishing up my survey."

"And you found nothing, right?"

Ruby hesitated to answer. She not only worked for Heath, she liked him quite a lot. Hell, she was about to be his date for New Year's Eve. Would divulging this information betray him in any way? Her immediate tendency was to protect him, however short their acquaintance had been. "The survey was inconclusive."

"Ah. I'm guessing you were hired by Heath Thurston?" Morgan reached out and straightened a blouse on a hanger. "What's he really like? I can't get a good read on him. Everyone says he's a jerk, including my fiancé. But I really like Nolan, Heath's twin. He and my sister Chelsea got married before Christmas and they're ridiculously happy. You should see the way he looks at her. You'd think she hung the moon. Identical twins are basically the same people, aren't they?"

Ruby was having a hard time keeping up. Morgan really liked to talk, and apparently she didn't have any qualms about discussing potentially sensitive matters in front of strangers. "I've never met Nolan, so I'm not sure I'm qualified to chime in on that. I do think twins can have different personalities. Especially if they've been through different things." Heath had mentioned that Nolan left Royal when he was eighteen and had stayed away until recently. She surmised that the brothers had grown apart even more during that time because Heath had hinted at efforts to mend their relationship. Her gut told her that Heath and Nolan were not identical in every regard. She'd have to assess that when she finally met Nolan on New Year's Eve.

Morgan tilted her head to one side. "I'm sorry. I'm rambling when I should be helping you. Are you in for something special today?"

"Actually, yes. I need a dress for New Year's Eve. I'm going to the party at the TCC."

"Oh! Nice!" Morgan's face lit up as she eyed Ruby from head to toe. "Girl, I've got a couple of things that would look amazing on you. Come on." With a wave of her hand, she invited Ruby to follow her back toward the front of the store.

In the corner, right in front of one of the large windows overlooking the street, was a sizable section of special occasion dresses. Ruby wasn't sure where to start, so she was glad Morgan was there to help her. "What do you suggest?"

"Something sparkly, of course. You've got to sparkle on New Year's Eve. It's like a rule." Morgan pulled out a silver-and-white sequined dress with a plunging neckline. It seemed like a huge leap from what Ruby was currently wearing—a pair of jeans, cowboy boots and yet another of her cozy sweaters.

"I'm not sure I feel like a sparkly person. At least, not now. Maybe something a little more subdued?"

Morgan shot Ruby a questioning glance. "We live in Royal, Texas, honey. You're going to the Texas Cattleman's Club on New Year's Eve. They might not let you in the door if you don't sparkle. Sparkly is the order of the day. Plus, you put on one of these dresses and you will see how amazing you look and you'll be ready to hand over your credit card. Trust me."

Ruby took in a deep breath. "Okay. But maybe not white. Maybe something darker?"

"Want something a little more mysterious?"

"I'd like it better if I wasn't visible from space."

Morgan laughed. "Got it." She flipped through the rack of dresses. "How about this?" She pulled out a deep emerald green full-length gown. It had skinny straps and the same plunging neckline of the previous dress, but Ruby felt like this one was a little more doable.

Ruby reached out and touched the fabric, which was surprisingly soft and silky in her hands. The sparkle came from threads woven into the cloth, rather than sequins. "I think this could work."

"Perfect. Let's try it on."

Ruby followed Morgan to the dressing room with a mix of excitement and nervousness. She hoped she was up to wearing this dress. It would make her night with Heath far more fun if she could pull it off. After their false start the other night, she really wanted to show him that she could be comfortable in her own skin and completely on board with him touching hers.

Heath had most meetings with his lawyer, Albert Cortez, at Albert's office in downtown Royal. Albert always said it was better to discuss delicate matters in person, where all parties could be more open about their opinions and no one had to worry about a paper trail. After Heath's chat with his brother yesterday, the question of whether to keep Albert on retainer seemed even more urgent to answer. Heath had to make a choice one way or the other.

"Heath, come on in. Have a seat." Albert eagerly waved Heath into his office. He was a stout man with a thick mustache that reminded Heath of a scrubbing brush. Heath had known him forever. Albert had been friends with his parents and was a strong tie to the past. "What can I help you with today? Have you made a decision?" Albert had a warm personality, but he didn't engage in much chitchat. It was always right down to business.

Heath parked himself in one of the leather armchairs opposite Albert's desk. "I'm afraid I don't know. Not until we talk about the one detail I think you missed."

Albert cocked a thick eyebrow at Heath and plopped down into his seat. "I'm all ears."

"It's the date on the original oil survey on the Grandin and Lattimore properties. Did you not notice that it was completed one year before my mother was given those oil rights?"

Deep creases formed between Albert's eyes. "Are you sure?"

"Ruby Bennett, the woman who did my survey,

told me. I haven't seen the original survey. I only heard about the results, and I heard about them from you."

"Well, let me see." Albert hoisted himself out of his chair and ambled over to an old wood filing cabinet. He flipped through the files in the top drawer, humming as he went. "Hold on. Your file is here somewhere."

That was not entirely reassuring, but Heath couldn't bear to give Albert a hard time. The man was kind and had a near encyclopedic knowledge of the law, especially as it pertained to oil rights.

"Here we go." Albert returned to his desk, put on a pair of reading glasses and flipped through what was a remarkably thin file. Had Heath made something out of nothing? Judging by the paltry number of documents, he was certainly wondering. "It's right here. And yes, you're right. One year. Almost to the day."

Heath blew out a frustrated breath, then sat forward and reached for the file. He needed to see it himself, but the confirmation only made him that much angrier. All he could do was imagine Victor Grandin Sr. and Augustus Lattimore signing that worthless piece of paper and presenting it to his mother as though it was of great value. "What do you suggest?"

Albert sat back in his chair and shrugged. "It really depends on your goals. And before you reply, let me remind you that revenge is not a goal. At least, not from a legal standpoint."

"I know that." Heath shifted in his seat, feeling uncomfortable. "What about a lawsuit, though? Based on the merits of those documents?"

"What are you going to do with more money, Heath? I already know you don't spend it on yourself, aside from maybe buying a new car every year."

"I'd like to fund an endowment for Ashley's foundation and get a therapeutic riding center off the ground. I've spoken to Lexi Alderidge-Bowden over at Alderidge Bank. She works extensively with nonprofits and she walked me through the specifics. It would mean that I could not only set it all up, but it would outlive me. I would never have to wonder whether Ashley's dream had been fulfilled."

"That is completely doable. And realistic. Although, I also know that you could fund an endowment on your own, right?"

"Well, sure, but I plan on paying to build everything. And it's the principle of the thing. Ashley spent her entire life being a good person and trying to make the world a better place. She could have done even more good if the Grandins had acknowledged that she was part of that family and given her everything she was entitled to."

Albert nodded. "Of course. Whatever you decide to do, I'm here for you. I just need you to give me the go-ahead and I'll start drafting a suit."

Heath glanced out the window. The sun was shining as bright as could be. His mind immediately went to Ruby. She was an unexpected bright spot. Despite his bluster when they'd first met in person, Ruby had been patient with him. She'd listened. And she seemed to understand what he was struggling with. That alone had been enough to dial down his anger and frustration about the oil rights. And then she kissed him, and, well, that had been enough to make him think harder about what he wanted for himself. Everyone in Royal assumed that he was hounding the Grandins and Lattimores because he enjoyed stirring up trouble. That couldn't be further from the truth. He longed to leave it all behind and move forward. Ruby only made that desire feel a bit more urgent. "Let me think on it, okay?" Heath rose from his seat and reached over to shake hands with Albert.

"Of course."

"I'd like to extend your retainer for another three months, if that works."

"Anything for you. And I appreciate the business. Just let me know what you decide to do."

Heath walked outside and decided to take advantage of the beautiful weather with a stroll down the main drag of Royal. Every step was another reminder of the past, especially when he passed people and they shot him glances and mumbled under their breath. Funny how this town had been home for his entire life, and he'd always been content here.

He'd never had a desire to get away. He'd spent years completely dumbfounded by his brother's decision to leave Royal behind. Now that he'd been forced to wrangle with some of the more unpleasant forces in this town, he could understand a little better why Nolan had stayed away.

A block or so into his walk, he caught a glimpse of something out of the corner of his eye that made him stop dead in his tracks. A blonde woman. Was that Ruby? In the Rancher's Daughter? The woman in question wasn't fully visible—he could only see a sliver of her between the clothing displays, and the view was of her back, but the hair looked to be the same. Her height, creamy skin and posture all made him think it was definitely her. But the dress this woman was wearing was the sticking point—it was so sexy it made his head spin, clinging to every inch of her appealing frame. It was also far more formal and dressy than anything he'd seen Ruby wear.

He stepped closer to the shop window for a better look, and that was when she turned to the side and he definitely knew it was her. His heart broke into an inconvenient sprint, making his pulse race. Why was he feeling like this? He'd only known her for a few days. Of course, it didn't take a rocket scientist to figure it out. She was smart, beautiful and kind—everything Heath admired in a woman. It would be so easy to get lost in her. His vision went fuzzy at the thought of touching her again. Kissing her.

Just then, another woman popped into view, and his stomach sank. He would've known that red hair anywhere. It was Morgan Grandin, the youngest of the Grandin kids. It wasn't a big surprise that she was there—it was her shop, after all. But it still put Heath on edge. Like every other time he'd seen Morgan, her mouth was moving at full speed. What in the world was she saying to Ruby?

He sucked in a deep breath, wondering about his next step, when Ruby turned toward the window and spotted him. Her eyes flickered and an effortless smile bloomed on her face. She waved. And that left Heath with no choice. He had to go talk to her. He pulled on the door and an electronic chime sounded as he walked into the boutique. He immediately headed in Ruby's direction.

"Speak of the devil," Ruby said, standing next to Morgan. "We were just talking about you."

Dammit. His worst suspicions were true. Morgan had been running her mouth about him. He could only imagine what she'd said. *You're going out on New Year's Eve with Heath Thurston? He's bad news, Ruby. Pure evil.* It wasn't a stretch. Her family not only hated him, Morgan's fiancé, Ryan, had gotten downright ugly about Heath's crusade over the oil rights. He'd confronted Heath at Chelsea and Nolan's wedding, for God's sake. These people were so predictable—if money and pride were involved, they'd drop down into the dirt and fight like hell rather than admit they'd done something wrong.

It would have been so easy to tear into Morgan. Heath had real ammunition against the Grandins now. But he wasn't ready to show his cards, and he certainly would not sink to the level of a Grandin. Not today. Not in front of Ruby. Heath sidled up to her. To his great surprise, Ruby gripped his biceps and kissed his cheek. It was a sweet gesture, but it made his blood run hot. "So that's why my ears were burning." He nodded at Morgan. "Hello, Morgan." It took everything he had to keep the venom out of his mouth when he said her name.

"Hey there, Heath. Funny that you should show up. Have you ever been in my store before?"

"I have not."

"I'm just doing a little shopping." Ruby's eyes darted back and forth between Morgan and him as she clearly tried to assess whether somebody was about to kick up some dirt. "I need something to wear for the New Year's party at the TCC. I don't have anything that's good enough for a place like that." She turned back to face the mirror, turning and twisting in front of it and eyeing herself.

Heath was blown away that she was making plans for their date, and so soon after he'd asked her, although he supposed the clock was ticking. The thirty-first would be here in two days. "I don't know what else you've tried on, but that dress looks spectacular."

"This is the first one. Morgan picked it out. I can't believe how perfect it is."

Morgan slid him a smile, which on the surface gave him some far more positive feelings about her, but he also had to wonder if she was happy merely because his approval meant she'd make a big sale.

"The dress is great, but you're what makes it special." Heath swallowed hard, wondering if he was laying it on too thick. He didn't want to mess things up with Ruby. Or put any undue pressure on her. She'd been through a lot.

Ruby looked down at herself, then turned her attention to him. "Do you really like it?"

Like was a wholly inadequate word. "I'll be with the most stunning woman in the room."

"Oh. Wow," Morgan said. "Okay. *Now* I'm putting the pieces together."

Ruby turned to her. "Pieces?"

Morgan cleared her throat and looked down at the floor for a moment. "I'm sorry. Sometimes words just fly out of my mouth." She stepped closer to Ruby and adjusted one of the straps of the dress. "I didn't realize that Heath was your date for New Year's. I thought we were just talking about him."

Heath's instinct to get into it with Morgan returned with a vengeance. He knew he was the subject of gossip in town, but the fact that Morgan was so willing to engage in it while fulfilling her role as shop owner? Apparently some members of the

Grandin family saw dragging his name through the mud as an everyday activity, like casually chatting about the weather.

"I'm sorry. I thought I'd told you," Ruby said.

"Don't worry about me. It's none of my business," Morgan said. "For what it's worth, I do think you two make a very cute couple."

Heath watched as Ruby's face flushed with pink, which was a pleasant distraction as he wondered if he was letting paranoia get the best of him. Or was Morgan simply buttering them up? Once again, the motivations of the Grandin family made him question everything.

"Thank you," Ruby said, then looked at Heath in the reflection of the mirror. "Well? Do you think I should get this one?"

"Even if you didn't have a big party to attend, I think it'd be foolish to not buy it. You look gorgeous."

From across the shop, a phone rang. "Oh, shoot. I left my cell by the register," Morgan said. "Please excuse me. I'm waiting on a call. I'll leave you two to talk about the dress." She bustled away.

Ruby took the price tag in her hand and looked at it, then once again peered into the mirror. "I'm not sure this is the best choice. Maybe I should be a little more sensible and buy something that I can wear more than once. I don't know where I would ever wear this after New Year's Eve."

He could hear the depth of her inner struggle in

her voice. Something told him this was about more than the dress. It was about her feeling unsure of herself. Heath so identified with that. There was something about loss that made you question everything you did. Everything that you were. "Then let me be the insensible one." He stepped closer to her. Everything in his mind and body made him want to touch her. Pull her into his arms.

"No offense, but I really don't think this dress would look good on you." She jokingly arched both eyebrows at him. "You don't have the hips to fill it out."

Heath laughed. "You know that wasn't what I was saying. Let me buy it for you."

"You haven't even looked at the price. This thing is expensive."

"I don't care about that. I care about you feeling good about yourself at this party. I care about you having fun that night. With me."

"That's so sweet."

If only she knew the thoughts that were going through his head right now. Not all of them were sweet. He wanted to wish Morgan away. He wanted to pull Ruby into the dressing room, lock the door, and kiss her and touch every inch of her until neither of them could see straight. "Is that a yes? Will you let me buy you the dress?"

"I don't know. It's a lot to ask."

He shook his head. "Trust me. You'd be doing me the favor."

"How, exactly?"

"It'll let me show a Grandin that I'm not a jerk. And it'll let me show you that, even though we haven't known each other for a very long time, I care."

She smiled softly and nodded, but it was clear that his words were still running through her head. "Okay, but on one condition. You let me take you out for lunch at the Royal Diner after this."

Heath's day was getting better at every turn. "Pie?"

"Of course," Ruby said.

Morgan returned. "Well? Do we have a decision?"

Heath pulled his credit card out of his wallet and handed it over to Morgan. "Sold."

"Yes, sir," she said in response. "Is there anything else you need, Ruby? Shoes? A handbag? A wrap?"

Heath didn't wait for Ruby to respond. "Whatever she wants."

Twenty minutes later, Heath and Ruby were leaving the Rancher's Daughter with two large shopping bags full of everything she needed for their night at the TCC. They walked down the street to the Royal Diner and popped inside. Heath hadn't crossed that threshold in quite some time. In general, he avoided it. The diner, with its red faux leather booths and black-and-white checkerboard floor, was an immensely popular spot in Royal, but that also made it a hub for gossip. He hoped they could have lunch in peace.

They were seated at a booth in the back, which gave them some semblance of privacy. "Thank you. For the dress and everything else. You really didn't have to do that." Ruby reached across the table and touched the back of his hand. "I appreciate it."

"I wanted to do it. Don't think twice about it." Heath perused the menu, realizing that one thing was still bothering him. "What were you and Morgan talking about before I got there?"

"You mean about you?"

He knew exactly how paranoid it made him seem, but he had to know. "I'm curious."

"It didn't take her long to figure out who I was. As soon as I told her that I'd been on her family's property, she knew that I worked for you. That's how we got on the subject. I assure you that I didn't simply pop into her store and start talking about you."

"Of course not. I wasn't thinking that you would do that. I assumed she was the instigator."

Ruby dropped her head to one side, admonishing him with a single glance. "If you want to know the truth, she said that she's not sure how you could possibly be the bad guy everyone makes you out to be."

"That's not a huge comfort."

"You don't actually care what people think, do

you? If you did, it seems like you would drop the whole thing."

He had to think about that for a moment. He'd told himself all along that he would never drop it. That it would be *wrong* to let it go. But that had been when he was walking around town with a big wall around himself, a wall that Ruby had managed to breach in short order. Now he was doing things he wouldn't have done a few months ago, like going to the Royal Diner and a New Year's Eve party at the TCC. He *did* care. At least a little. "Popular opinion isn't a reason to walk away from something that's difficult."

"Heath, you really should tell people about the foundation. Tell them how much good you want to do for others. And for this community. That will turn around their opinion of you."

"Why? Does that somehow make this battle morally correct?" He leaned closer so he could whisper. "The two women I cared about most in this world were deceived and tricked by powerful people who had nothing to lose other than a bit of money and pride. That gives me plenty of moral high ground." With every word, he felt his blood pressure rising and his face growing hot. His anger hadn't lessened because of Ruby. It had only been blurred. "It's the Grandins and the Lattimores who need to think about what's good and bad. More often than not, they're on the wrong side of that equation."

Ruby scanned his face, her eyes sweeping back and forth. "Okay."

Her tone of voice told him everything. He'd gone too far. "I'm sorry." He willed himself to calm down. Maybe everyone in town was right. Maybe he really was a jerk.

"I understand, Heath. I do. My guess is you're going to have to find a way to put all of this to rest."

He reached across the table and took her hand, marveling at how soft her skin was. "Let's talk about New Year's Eve. And you in that dress."

"What's there to say about that?"

"Only that I can't wait for the moment when we walk in the front door with you on my arm."

She smiled. "You really are a total flirt. I need to run to the ladies' room. Order me a cheeseburger when the waitress comes."

"Got it." He watched her walk away from the table. Her words were still tumbling in his head. *Put all of this to rest.* He needed to do that. For himself. For the sake of his growing relationship with Ruby. He just needed to exhaust the one detail that wouldn't go away. Then he could wash his hands of the whole thing. He'd know in his heart that he had done everything he could to make things right for the memories of his mom and sister. He pulled his phone out of his pocket and sent a text to Albert. Send the letters. Let them know that I know.

His response came quickly. You sure?

Heath imagined what would come next—surely drama, especially from the Grandins. But it would pass quickly, they would finally pay, and then he could move on. Yes. I'm sure.

Six

Ruby was filled with a mix of nerves and optimism. It was an odd cocktail to kick off her New Year's Eve, but she couldn't do anything about the way she was feeling. The reality was that she still didn't know what to make of Heath. She liked him so much that it scared her at times, but there was a temper locked up inside his handsome head and she didn't like the way it came out when she wasn't expecting it. Case in point, their conversation at the Royal Diner two days ago. One minute, everything was fine, and then the next minute, he was spewing vitriol about the Grandin and Lattimore families. It wasn't good for her to be around that kind of negativity, and she wasn't sure what it would take for him to move beyond it.

But she also felt as though she'd gotten through to him. He'd listened to her. He seemed to appreciate that she understood him on a deeper level. They had both been through so much. That commonality had forged their connection from the very beginning. How rare a thing that was—to feel a real bond so soon after meeting someone. She couldn't cast that aside or ignore it. Something in the very center of her heart told her that she had to explore where this might go, even if there might be moments that made her nervous.

For now, Ruby was standing in her foyer, looking out through the sidelights next to her front door, waiting for Heath to pick her up for the party. As soon as she saw the headlights coming up the driveway, she gathered her evening bag, draped her faux fur wrap around her shoulders and walked out onto the front porch, then locked her front door.

"Ruby!" Heath called from behind her. "You should have let me come to the door to get you."

She turned and watched as he stepped into the glow of her porch lights. Good Lord, the man could rock a tuxedo like no one she'd ever seen. The relaxed and genuine smile on his face told her that everything she'd been worrying about earlier was silly.

"I'm fine," she said as she descended the staircase.

"That's not the point." He held out his hand for

her. "Call me old-fashioned, but I feel like I owe it to you to pick you up at your door."

She hooked her arm in his as they walked across the driveway. He hadn't driven his truck this time, but had instead brought some sort of fancy sports car. "Next time I'll wait inside. How about that?"

"As long as there's a next time, I'm happy." He opened the passenger's-side car door for her. "You look stunning, by the way," he said as she slid into the seat.

"You don't look half bad yourself."

"Perfect. That's exactly what I was going for. Not half bad." He closed her door and rounded the back of the vehicle, then climbed into the driver's seat, turned on the car and started down her driveway to the main road. "So, tonight. I want you to know that we can leave anytime you want. If this isn't your scene or you aren't having fun, just tell me. I don't have any strong feelings one way or the other as to how long we stay."

"It sounds to me like you do, though."

"You know how it is in Royal. People talk. And I'm sure a few people are going to choose to talk about me tonight. That might not be fun for you, and I want you to have a good time. It's the only thing I really care about."

Ruby reached over and touched his arm. "Don't worry about me. I'm looking forward to meeting your brother and sister-in-law and getting to know each other. That's all *I* really care about."

He slid her an approving glance. "You are amazing. I hope you know that."

She grinned and settled back a little more in her seat. "Thanks. That's really nice to hear."

About twenty minutes later, they pulled into the parking lot of the Texas Cattleman's Club. There were already hundreds of cars there, and the windows of the sprawling single-story slate-topped building were all lit up. Outside, dozens of couples were approaching the entrance to the imposing dark stone-and-wood structure.

"Wow," Ruby said. "I've driven past here, but only during the day. I've never seen it at night. It really is impressive."

Heath pulled into a parking space and killed the engine. "I suppose it is. I guess I never gave it much thought."

"Have you been a member for a long time?"

"Our family have been members my entire life. My father became a member before Nolan and I were born. It helped him network when he was trying to put the Thurston ranch on the map."

"Huh. Interesting."

"Why is that interesting?"

"Because you always talk about yourself as a Royal outsider. But being a member of the Texas

Cattleman's Club for your entire life sort of disproves that theory, doesn't it?"

"It's a club. A way to do business."

"Well, sure, but not everyone belongs, do they? It's still an elite and exclusive circle."

Heath looked off through the windows of his car. "Interesting. I never thought of it that way."

"That's what happens. We get used to something and don't think anything of it. But to someone else, it might seem like a big deal." She clapped him on the shoulder. "I, for one, am excited that you're a member. It means I finally get to experience it for myself."

They climbed out of the car, and Ruby hooked her arm in Heath's as they strode through the parking lot. There was excitement in the air as he opened one of the tall doors for her and they stepped inside to the impressive entry, with its soaring ceilings and opulent furnishings. Hunting trophies and historic artifacts seemed to adorn every wall. The space was abuzz with the sound of celebratory conversation, filled to the hilt with people. Ruby's first impression was that the Texas Cattleman's Club was a place built on money and longevity, much like Royal itself.

As they made their way toward the reception table, Ruby immediately spotted Nolan, who was impossible to miss given that he was the spitting image of Heath. Standing next to Nolan was a tall and willowy woman with flowing dark brown hair, wearing a strapless black dress, who Ruby could only presume was Chelsea.

Nolan spotted Heath and Ruby as they approached and waved. "Well, well, well. You actually showed up." He extended his arm and shook hands with Heath, then immediately turned to Ruby. "You must be Ruby. I've heard a lot about you."

She eyed Heath, who looked embarrassed. "Really? I wasn't aware there was much to say."

"Don't be modest," Heath interjected, then turned to his brother. "And don't make me look bad, okay? It's our first real date."

A wave of heat rushed across her skin. She liked hearing him describe their night out as a date. She offered her hand to Chelsea. "Hi. I'm Ruby. You must be Chelsea."

"I am. I heard a lot about you, too. From my sister, Morgan." Chelsea shook Ruby's hand and smiled warmly, putting Ruby at ease. "The dress is fabulous, by the way."

"Thank you." Ruby wasn't used to having so much focus on her. "Can we go inside and get a drink?"

Nolan looked at Heath with sly regard. "I like her already."

The four of them filed into the grand ballroom where the party was set to take place. Straight ahead, there was a large dance floor, which was already filled with people enjoying themselves. Black, silver and gold metallic streamers hung from the ceiling for festive effect, while dozens of large round tables dotted the perimeter of the room.

"Our table is over here." Chelsea led them through the crowd of people and to a spot on the far left. It was a bit quieter in this part of the room, but only by a slim margin. The party was definitely in full swing.

A waiter stopped by their table, delivering four glasses of champagne as they each took a seat. "I'd like to suggest a toast," Nolan said. "To new beginnings."

"Hear, hear." Ruby raised her glass and clinked it with everyone else's while she tried to gauge Heath's reaction to his brother's words. She hoped that he would soon start to realize that he could give himself his own new beginning, simply by looking forward.

Chelsea took a second sip of her champagne, then set her glass on the table. "Here comes my brother, Vic. Ruby, I believe you met him that day you were out on my family's property."

Ruby turned and instantly recognized the man, with his solid build and penetrating brown eyes, much like Chelsea's. She remembered very much the way he'd reacted when she'd been out on the Grandin property and hoped greatly that he wasn't about to confront her about it.

As if he understood what she was feeling, Heath reached over and gently grasped her forearm. "If he's a jerk to you, please let me take the heat," he whispered in her ear.

"I can handle it on my own," she muttered in return.

"I have no doubt about that. I'm only saying that I'm willing to take the bullet."

"Hello, everyone," Vic said, leaning down to kiss his sister on the cheek.

Nolan stood and shook hands with Vic. "Happy New Year, Vic."

"It'd be a little happier if you hadn't brought your twin," Vic said.

"Vic. Please don't start this," Chelsea pleaded, getting up from her seat.

Heath got up, too. "Chelsea, you don't need to defend me. I know Vic doesn't like me."

"And yet that has done nothing to change your behavior," Vic shot back.

Ruby watched the two men stare each other down, her heart pounding.

"I don't need your approval," Heath said. "But I'm sure you've figured that out by now."

Vic glanced at Ruby, then directed his stare at Heath again. "I see you brought your surveyor this evening. I still can't believe you sent a woman to do your dirty work."

"Shut the hell up," Heath blurted, then lunged for Vic.

Nolan got between them in the nick of time. "Hold on, you two." He was facing his brother, with Vic at his back. "It's a party. Please don't ruin this. Let's try to get along."

"Talk to your brother," Vic groaned. "And don't worry about me. I'll spend the rest of the night on the other side of the room." He turned to Chelsea. "'Bye, sis. I'll see you later." Just as quickly as he'd arrived, Vic stalked off.

Chelsea rushed over to Ruby. "I am so sorry. My brother can be a real hothead."

Ruby shook her head. "It's okay. Honestly, I'm only mad that I didn't have a chance to tell him off. I realize you're related to him, but that thing he said about being a woman was pretty sexist. I can hold my own."

Chelsea blew out a frustrated breath. "Yeah. He can be extremely misogynistic. I usually call him on it, but I was hoping tonight could have a minimum of family drama."

Heath was right at her side, eyes full of concern. "Are you okay?"

His question made her want to laugh. It also made her want to kiss him. "Are you? You're the one who nearly got into a fight."

He stroked her arm up and down with the tips of his fingers, bringing her entire body to life. "It's not a big deal. I'm fine. I only want to be sure that you're okay."

Ruby smiled and leaned in to kiss his cheek. His

concern and protective nature were so endearing. "I promise you that I'm more than okay. I'm great."

He planted his hand on her hip and curled his fingers into her bottom. "Oh, I already knew that."

She laughed quietly. "You're flirting again."

"I'll keep doing what works until it stops being effective."

"Hey, Ruby," Chelsea said. "I'm going to run to the ladies' room. Do you want to come with me?"

Ruby felt torn. What she really wanted was to fall into Heath's arms. But maybe it was a good idea for her to cool off. It was going to be a long night. "Sure thing." She turned to Heath. "We'll be right back."

"I'll be waiting."

Heath watched as Ruby and Chelsea left for the ladies' room. "Any clue what they're going to talk about?" he asked Nolan.

"Us, of course." Nolan flagged down a waiter. "Any chance we can get two bourbons, neat?"

"Absolutely, sir. I'll be right back." The waiter disappeared into the crowd.

"Smart thinking," Heath said, taking his seat again. "I could use something stronger than champagne."

Nolan joined him. "I figured as much. I'm sorry that happened. Vic can be a great guy, but he can also be a jerk."

Heath shrugged. "He's protecting his family. Just like I am. So I figure we're even."

Nolan nodded and drew in a deep breath through

his nose. "I'm glad you decided to come tonight. I feel bad that I shut you down the other day when you called and you wanted to talk."

"Really? What happened to being absolutely sure that you didn't want to talk about the oil rights?"

"I don't want to talk about it. Ever. But I feel stuck. Between you and Chelsea."

Heath let that tumble around in his head. He didn't want his brother to suffer, but maybe it was good for Nolan to feel stuck. Heath had felt that way for his entire life. "Chelsea and I are fine. I like her. She likes me. We don't talk about her family. It seems to work."

Nolan leaned forward and rested his elbow on the table, casting Heath a serious look. "I have to wonder how long that's sustainable."

"It'll go away soon. And then we can all move on." Heath hadn't told Nolan that he'd asked Albert to file the suit against the Grandin estate. His brother had made it clear that he wanted to be kept in the dark when it came to that matter, and Heath was committed to keeping that promise. Still, he eventually wanted Nolan to know about the timing of the original survey and the issuance of the oil rights to their mother. A lawsuit, or the threat of one, might be the only way to bring that final and crucial detail to light.

A slight smile broke across Nolan's face. "I'm glad to hear you say that. Really glad."

"I'd like to talk about Ashley's foundation. About the riding center. I've contacted an architect and he's set to come for a site visit in a few days."

"That's fantastic you've gotten the ball rolling." Nolan knocked Heath's shoulder with his fist just as the waiter dropped off their drinks. He slipped the waiter a ten, then raised his glass. "To making Ashley's dream come true."

Heath clinked his glass with his brother's. "I'd really like you to be involved. In all of it. It will mean more if we do this together."

"Absolutely. You can count on me. Whatever you need."

"Count on you for what?" Chelsea asked as she and Ruby appeared back at the table.

Nolan stood and took her hand. "A trip around the dance floor, of course." He turned back to Heath and Ruby. "We'll see you two in a little bit."

Ruby eased into her seat. "They're adorable together. They seem really happy."

They did seem happy. Heath wondered if he would ever feel like that. Ruby certainly made him believe that it was possible. "Would you like to dance?"

She winced and made a funny face. "I sort of have two left feet."

"It's okay. We'll go slow." He stood and grasped her hand, tugging her closer to the dance floor. He wound his way through the crowd, ignoring anyone who cast him a disparaging look. He was going to dance with his date and that was all there was to that. As soon as they were out there with the other couples, Heath wasted no time pulling Ruby into his arms.

"You don't really seem like the dancing type," she said.

He laughed, noticing how easily she pressed into him and warmed him from head to toe. "I'm not. But I love music, and I would have to be a fool to not want everyone in Royal to see me with the most beautiful woman at this party."

She shook her head. "You heap entirely too much praise on me."

"Not true. In fact, I get the distinct impression that you don't get enough praise and attention in your life. I worry about you living down that road, all by yourself."

"I know. It wasn't that smart for me to buy my place, but I wanted a fixer-upper and that was the cheapest thing I could find."

He disliked the thought of her having to worry about money, but he supposed that was part and parcel of being in her line of work. It certainly couldn't be lucrative. "So you fixed up the whole thing by yourself?"

"I did. I worked through my grief by knocking down walls and ripping up old tile and putting in new light fixtures. The whole nine yards."

"I can't believe you didn't hire someone to do it."

"It was a learning experience. I wanted to push my limits. So I sanded those floors on my hands and knees, chipping away at it a little more every day. It took forever. Which is why I was so mad when you wouldn't take your boots off."

"I eventually succumbed to your requests."

Her eyes had a sexy glimmer. "And my kiss. You succumbed to that, too."

He turned her in a circle, and the whole room fell away. Despite the negativity that had been aimed at him this evening, none of it came close to matching the positive charge of being with Ruby. "Of course I did. I'd been thinking about it for hours."

"You had?"

"Pretty much from the moment I laid eyes on you."

She swallowed so hard that he saw the motion in her graceful neck. "What were you thinking?"

He pulled her even closer and swept her hair aside so he could speak right into her ear. "I was thinking that if I could convince you to kiss me, I would be the luckiest guy in the world. I was thinking that I wanted to touch you and taste you and explore every inch of your beautiful body."

Ruby audibly sighed. "And I disappointed you."

"No. You didn't. It's not possible for you to disappoint me. I'm glad we waited. And we can wait as long as you want to." It wasn't an easy thing to say, but he meant it. He was fully committed to following her lead.

"What if I said that I was thinking about you from the moment I met you?"

That admission made everything below his waist draw tight. "Really?" His voice came out raspy and raw.

"Yes, really. I almost kissed you in the driveway when I fell."

"Seriously? I was acting like a person with half a brain."

She shrugged. "It was endearing. That you cared that much. Most people don't care about anything outside themselves. You do. It's very sexy."

"When else did you think about kissing me?"

"In my room, when we went to get the mattress. I almost pushed you down on the bed right then and there and begged you to take me."

Not only was this conversation making Heath's blood run hot, it was making him feel so damn lucky. That instant attraction he'd felt went both ways. "I would never make you beg."

"Not even a little?"

A lustful groan rumbled around in the base of his throat, and he found his head drifting closer to hers. He wanted to kiss her so bad it hurt. "I'm not saying it wouldn't turn me on." *Just like this whole conversation. Just like everything about you.*

Ruby leaned in and nudged his cheek with her

FREE BOOKS GIVEAWAY

2 FREE SIZZLING ROMANCE BOOKS!

2 FREE PASSIONATE ROMANCE BOOKS!

GET UP TO FOUR FREE BOOKS & TWO FREE GIFTS WORTH OVER $20!

We pay for everything!

YOU pick your books –
WE pay for everything.
You get up to FOUR New Books and TWOMystery Gifts...absolutely FREE!

Dear Reader,

I am writing to announce the launch of a huge **FREE BOOKS GIVEAWAY**... and to let you know that YOU are entitled to choose up to FOUR fantastic books that WE pay for.

Try **Harlequin® Desire** books featuring the worlds of the American elite with juicy plot twists, delicious sensuality and intriguing scandal.

Try **Harlequin Presents® Larger-Print** books featuring the glamourous lives of royals and billionaires in a world of exotic locations, where passion knows no bounds.

Or **TRY BOTH!**

In return, we ask just one favor: Would you please participate in our brief Reader Survey? We'd love to hear from you.

This FREE BOOKS GIVEAWAY means that your introductory shipment is completely free, <u>even the shipping</u>! If you decide to continue, you can look forward to curated monthly shipments of brand-new books from your selected series, always at a discount off the cover price! <u>Plus you can cancel any time</u>. Who could pass up a deal like that?

Sincerely

Pam Powers

Pam Powers
For Harlequin Reader Service

Complete the survey below and return it today to receive up to 4 FREE BOOKS and FREE GIFTS guaranteed!

FREE BOOKS GIVEAWAY
Reader Survey

1

Do you prefer stories with happy endings?

◯ YES ◯ NO

2

Do you share your favorite books with friends?

◯ YES ◯ NO

3

Do you often choose to read instead of watching TV?

◯ YES ◯ NO

YES! Please send me my Free Rewards, consisting of **2 Free Books** from each series I select and **Free Mystery Gifts**. I understand that I am under no obligation to buy anything, no purchase necessary see terms and conditions for details.

❑ **Harlequin Desire®** (225/326 HDL GRK3)
❑ **Harlequin Presents® Larger-Print** (176/376 HDL GRK3)
❑ **Try Both** (225/326 & 176/376 HDL GRLF)

| FIRST NAME | LAST NAME |

| ADDRESS | |

| APT.# | CITY |

| STATE/PROV. | ZIP/POSTAL CODE |

EMAIL ❑ Please check this box if you would like to receive newsletters and promotional emails from Harlequin Enterprises ULC and its affiliates. You can unsubscribe anytime.

nose, her breath hot against his skin. Then she inched closer to his ear. "Please tell me you want me. Tell me now."

"I want you," he muttered. "Now."

"You're going to have to wait. We're at a New Year's Eve party and it's not even eight o'clock. Don't you want to ring in the New Year?"

Heath felt as though his head was swimming. He couldn't see straight. All he could think about was being alone with Ruby. "Here's the problem."

"Okay…"

"We wait until midnight. Which is going to be hard for me because, right now, I want you so bad that I can barely form coherent sentences."

"I don't know. You're doing pretty well for yourself right now."

He laughed, which at least helped to loosen the tension in his body. "Just listen a second." He pulled her even closer, flattening his hand against the center of her back and holding her flush against him, if only to soak up more of her body heat. "The problem is that I'm going to kiss you when the clock strikes twelve. And once that happens, I'm not going to want to stop. And as much as I would love to give this town some more to say about me, they'd start saying those things about you, too, and I can't live with that."

She bit down on her lip, staring up into his eyes.

"You are a mystery to me, Heath Thurston, but I do love watching your mind at work."

"So? Can I convince you to skip the countdown to midnight and come back to my place now?"

She unleashed half a grin, eased up onto her toes and planted a soft, wet kiss on his lips. "I've been waiting all night for you to ask."

Seven

Ruby felt as though her entire body was on fire. Heath was that hot. And she wanted him that badly. At any other time in her life, this might have been the perfect time to start thinking about nonsexy things, if only to force herself to cool down a bit. But she didn't want to douse the flames inside her. Not this time. They made her feel alive. She didn't want to keep pressing Pause on her own existence. So, for tonight, she'd focus on kindling the blaze.

"This is us," Heath said as he turned off the main road. They were far away from where Ruby lived, in one of the parts of Royal where the parcels of land grew impossibly large, cattle roamed the rolling hills, and the sprawling homes were often as grand as they were expensive. This was a place of permanence, reminding Ruby of Heath's ties to this town, which was ironically where Ruby had gone when she needed to start over.

As they got closer to Heath's place, the house came into view. It was an impressive property, clad in river stone with a tall pitched roof above the center porch and entrance, which hosted double glass-paned doors and a circular wrought-iron chandelier. It struck her that this was where almost all of Heath's history had been written, the past that still haunted him. She hoped that crossing the threshold would mean that she could better understand him. "It's beautiful, Heath. Absolutely gorgeous."

"Thanks," he said as he clicked a button on the dash of his car and eased the vehicle into the three-bay garage. "It's home. The only one I've ever known." He shut off the engine and turned to her. "Ready to see it?"

"It's so wonderful that you've lived here your entire life. I've moved around too much over the years."

"Staying in one place isn't all it's cracked up to be." He led her inside, through a mudroom and into the kitchen, which was nearly the size of Ruby's entire cottage. It had beautiful black Shaker cabinets, white marble countertops with gray veining, and a wide porcelain farmhouse sink with a window above it overlooking the property. "And I'm sure you've been to all sorts of exciting places. You've probably traveled more than I have."

"I doubt it. I've never even been out of the state of Texas." It was a little embarrassing to admit, but she couldn't help but be honest. She took this chance to set her handbag and wrap on the kitchen table, which was situated in a large bay of windows.

"You should let me take you somewhere." He reached for her and ran his fingers down the back of her bare arm as he admired her, which made her feel as though she was floating above the floor.

"Like where?"

He shrugged and clasped one of her hands. Then the other. "Anywhere you want."

"New York?"

"Sure." He slyly grinned and tugged her a little closer.

"San Francisco? Miami?"

"Of course."

Heath was offering to open up the world for her, which was such a generous gesture. If only he could understand how she felt about it—part of her wanted nothing more than to strike out on an adventure, but there was another part that craved the reliable comforts of home. A home like this one that felt as though it was never going anywhere. "Your bedroom?"

A low groan left his throat and he pulled her closer. "I thought you'd never ask." His lips fell on hers and there was this magical moment where she lost all sense of time and place, and nothing else existed other than Heath, his strong hands caressing her back, and the way his tongue sought hers in a warm and giving kiss. She did not have a care in the world right now and it buoyed her like nothing she'd experienced in a long time.

She popped up onto her tiptoes, stretched out her arms onto his shoulders and dug her fingers into his thick hair. She deepened their kiss, and he countered, making her whimper with desire. He wrapped his arms tighter around her, but then one hand dropped to her hip and gathered the skirt of her dress upward, taking a fistful of the garment. His fingers reached her bare thigh, and she gasped as though he'd just burned her, but it was the most pleasurable feeling she'd experienced in an eon. A man's touch. She needed more of it.

"I thought we were going to your bedroom," she said, breathless.

"Where are my manners?" With that, he reached down and swept her into his arms, holding her tight.

She wrapped her arms around his neck and set her head against his chest, craving his warmth and relishing the safety of his arms.

He wasted no time walking through the house and to his bedroom. He planted a knee on the bed and set her down gently. She kicked off her heels, then reclined and swished her hands across the duvet, which was soft and silky. "This feels amazing."

"You're amazing." Heath worked his shoulders out of his tuxedo jacket and yanked off his tie, not taking his eyes off her for so much as a second.

She couldn't stop looking at him either. The raw need on his face was fuel for her own desire. Knowing he wanted her gave her so much confidence. It made her feel bold. She propped up on her elbows and raised her knee, allowing the skirt of her dress to slide down her thigh to her hip. He responded by unbuttoning his shirt at lightning speed.

"I like watching you take your clothes off," she said, surprised she had the guts to do so.

He tossed his shirt on the floor. "I'm going to enjoy taking *your* clothes off." He stretched out on the bed next to her and kissed her like his life depended on it. He flattened her against the bed and she dug her fingers into his back, hitching her leg up over his hips and taking the back of his thigh with her foot. He was nothing but muscle, surely made from countless hours working on the ranch. She slipped her other leg between his and pressed against his crotch, feeling his erection and prompting a groan from the depths of his belly. The heat inside her was building like a wildfire on a hot and windy day. This was an all-new level of longing.

He pulled one dress strap off her shoulder and

she clamped her eyes shut, relishing his touch as he tugged down the other. "My zipper," she muttered.

Heath eased to his side and took Ruby with him, then drew down the metal closure until it was all the way past her waist. He tugged down the layers of fabric, and luckily, she didn't have to ask him to unhook the strapless bra the dress required. He did that all on his own, then cupped one of her breasts with his hand and rubbed her nipple with his thumb, which was deliciously rough and calloused. He lowered his head and flicked his tongue against the tight bundle of nerves, and she felt heat surge in her body, rushing to meet his lips as he drew her skin into his mouth. She moaned, rubbing her leg even harder against his steely length.

He lowered his hand and raked her skirt higher. When he reached her hip, he moved across her belly, and then his fingers slipped down into the front of her panties. He took his time reaching her center, teasing with a delicate touch that made her arch her back. One skilled loop with his fingers and she was digging her nails into his biceps, needing him to keep going. As he artfully rolled his fingertips over her clit, the pressure in her hips started building, and she knew it wouldn't take much for her to give way. She clamored for his belt buckle, unhooking it and unzipping his pants. Without so much as an instant of hesitation, she slipped her hand inside, molding her fingers around his erection, loving how hard and hot he was. All she could think about was what it would be like to have him inside her, to experience every magnificent inch of him.

Thankfully, he led the charge by scrambling off the bed and shucking his pants and boxers. Ruby quickly shifted to her knees and wriggled her dress and panties past her hips. Heath climbed back onto the mattress behind her. He took her hair in his hand and pulled it aside, wrapping his other arm around her waist and pulling her snug against his body. He ground his hips against her bottom as he kissed his way from the nape of her neck to one shoulder, then back to the center. Needing more of him, Ruby turned in his arms and planted a hot, wet kiss on his lips. Then she did what she'd never imagined herself doing. She pushed him back onto the bed. The shock on his face was its own reward. She loved the thought of surprising him.

Heath could not believe his own eyes. Hovering above him was naked Ruby, a curvy and sumptuous feast for every one of his senses. She dragged her hand down his chest and stomach, then shot him a white-hot look before gripping his erection, lowering her head and taking him into her mouth. His eyes clamped shut, his mouth so agape with pleasure that he wasn't sure he'd ever be able to close his jaw again. The tenderness of her tongue, the firm and careful grip of her lips, and the warmth of her mouth felt so impossibly good. It would've been amazing to have this treatment from any woman, but from Ruby, it went so far beyond physical gratification. He was a lucky man and he knew it.

Heath caressed Ruby's shoulders and combed his fingers through her silky hair over and over again, matching her steady rhythm. He let go of as many thoughts as he could, the things that worried him and stressed him out, and instead allowed himself the luxury of the pleasure Ruby was lavishing on him. But when she gripped his hips more firmly with her hands and rolled her tongue over the tip of his length, he knew he couldn't last too much longer. As heavenly as this was, it wasn't everything he really wanted.

He grasped her arms and tugged her closer. "Come here, Ruby. I need to kiss you."

She carefully relinquished her hold on him. "I'm right here." She began to crawl up the length of his body, pressing her lips along his midline, inch by inch. Heath smoothed his hands over the velvety skin of her butt, then along her spine, until she reached his neck and they could finally fall into the kiss he so desperately wanted. He cupped both sides of her face as their tongues wound in an endless loop. He could have kissed her forever, but then her knees dropped to the bed, bracketing his hips. That left her slick center riding along his dick as she ground into him.

His mind became a hazy place. His belly drew tight and he was right back on the precipice of release.

"Condom," he muttered. "Let me get one."

One more kiss, then Ruby rolled off him, allowing him to get up from the bed. As he opened the nightstand drawer and pulled out the box, she sprawled out on the bed, leaving him with the visual of her glorious body. She was slowly killing him, that was all there was to it, and that was a good thing. He didn't need much more in life than her right now. He tore open the foil packet and rolled it on himself quickly, never allowing himself to look away from her beauty.

She had the goofiest grin on her face, and in that moment, he fully appreciated just how much she already trusted him. He wished he could be like that, always seeing the good and looking away from the bad. He placed a knee on the bed, and she responded by spreading her legs wider, welcoming him as he positioned himself at her entrance and drove inside.

With that first stroke, Heath needed an instant to grapple with how perfectly they fit together. Her heat and grip on him were everything he could have asked for, and it made it hard to breathe. Made him work to think. He settled his weight on her and she wrapped her legs around his waist, dragging her heels along the backs of his thighs. He focused on every little noise she made, wanting this to be a mind-blowing experience. He not only needed to please her, he wanted to give himself the best chance at this happening again.

Their kisses were slow and deep while the pressure was coiling tightly inside him. He drove harder, listening to her breaths as they became choppier and the way she countered his strokes became more insistent. The pleasure was mounting, becoming impossible to resist, but he waited until her body clutched and she arched into him. Then he tumbled into his release, his shoulders and hips freezing and relaxing over and over again as he allowed the waves to wash over him.

A million kisses followed, and even then it didn't seem like it was enough. Eventually, Heath got up to use the bathroom, getting rid of the condom and washing his hands. Ruby took her turn right after him, and he waited in his bed for her, eager to wrap himself around her when she arrived.

"So, is it really true that you've never been out of Texas?" he asked. "You've never even taken a step over the state line?"

Ruby snuggled closer to him. "Why? Does that make me sound pathetic?"

"No. Of course not. I just want to know more about you. And, I mean, if you had to pick a state to live your whole life in, Texas would be a great choice."

"I guess I just never had the chance to go anywhere else. Either work was getting in the way, or money. Or sometimes, both."

He cleared his throat, wondering if it was wise to bring up the topic that was so present in his mind right now. It was the thing that had made her hold back the first time they were together. "Was Lucas from Texas?"

She paused for a moment, making him wonder if he'd made a grave mistake. "He was. Born and raised in Abilene. We met on a job site."

He considered asking for more, but discussing her former fiancé wasn't the best pillow talk. "I wasn't kidding when I told you that I'd take you someplace. We'd have fun traveling together." Heath couldn't even remember the last time he'd been on a vacation.

"How do I choose?" Ruby pushed up on her elbow and propped her head up with her hand. The moon outside was so bright that it cast her in the most mind-blowing glow. She really was so beautiful.

"Make a list. We'll do them all."

"How many places can I pick? I'd like to go to California. San Francisco and LA. I really want to go to New York City and Washington, DC, and Miami. And of course, I'd really love to go someplace like the Grand Canyon. It would be so much fun to go geek out on rocks for a week."

"I've been to a few of those places. Some are great. Some aren't all that. I loved New York the few times I've been. It's very, very different from Texas. Totally different from Royal."

"You've spent your whole life here, haven't you?"

"I have. Born and raised. Nolan was the one who got out, but not me. Someone had to stay and look after the ranch."

"Does that bother you? That you stayed and he took off?"

Just thinking about Nolan's departure made him sad. They were only eighteen at the time, and Heath already knew the ranch was his life. "It bothered me a lot when he first left. I was furious because he took off without warning. I couldn't understand how he could leave or why he wanted to. But we've talked a fair amount since he came back to town. I think I get it now." He drew in a deep breath. "You know, even though we're twins, we can be very different. I always felt like the one who had to be responsible for everything. I love the ranch, but there was always the pressure of making it into a success because I knew my dad was counting on me to look after everything and everyone."

"So when Nolan left, it felt like your fate was sealed?"

Heath drew his fingers up and down Ruby's spine. "I suppose I did. I definitely felt like a door closed." Had feeling stuck fueled his quest against the Grandin and Lattimore families? Had it given him too much time to think? Ruby made him ask himself these questions, but he kept it all to himself.

"I'm glad you stayed here. We might not have met otherwise. And I can't wait to see the ranch."

"I'll gladly give you a tour." The thought filled him with even more optimism. It was one more thing to look forward to, spending time with her and showing off the product of his hard work.

"I'd like that. I'd like to learn more about you, too."

Heath pulled her closer. "What are you going to do for your birthday?"

Ruby reared her head back. "How did you know my birthday was coming?"

"You told me the day I came to your house."

"I did?"

"Yes. Remember when I was trying to explain how I thought you might be older than you are?"

Ruby laughed quietly. "Oh, right. I forgot about that."

"Good. I keep playing that moment over in my head, hating myself for making the mistake."

"To answer your question, I don't have any plans. I honestly haven't done anything for three years. My brother tried to convince me to visit last year, but I just wasn't in the mood for celebrating."

"Would it be okay if you and I celebrated? I think it's a good idea." He wondered if he was pushing her too hard. He knew how much he disliked it when someone pressured him about anything.

"What did you have in mind?"

"Whatever you want. It's your birthday."

"Maybe dinner?"

"Of course. Where would you like to go?"

"Sheen? Is that too much to ask?"

Heath hesitated for a moment, because he knew exactly what going to Sheen involved. It was the hippest restaurant in all of Royal and, because of that, immensely popular. He'd been a few times, and it'd been packed to the rafters on every occasion. Would he receive the same treatment he'd just endured at the TCC? Would someone like Vic decide to take issue with him? Every passing day made it more likely. It wouldn't be long before the Grandin and Lattimore families would receive the letter from his lawyer, and then it would be their turn to put up or shut up. "Nothing is too much to ask. I'd love to take you to Sheen. I'll make a call and get a reservation."

Eight

Ruby was finally starting her last house project, a complete rework of the closet in her bedroom. Closets in older homes were notoriously tiny, and hers was bursting at the seams. The hanging clothes were so jam-packed that it took an extraordinary amount of upper body strength to pull a single hanger off the rod. The shoes were even worse—the entire floor was littered with a mountain of cowboy boots, sneakers, sandals and heels. Starting the project had created its own mess. Ruby's entire wardrobe was piled on the sofa in the living room to keep it away from the construction dust.

Her first task was to remove the drywall at the back of her closet, which gave her access to the same space in the guest room. It wasn't a load-bearing

wall, so she planned to knock down the framing between and double the square footage for her wardrobe. It was a big undertaking, but completing it
would mean that she was done with transforming her
house. Unless she thought of a new project. There
was always something that could be done to improve
things. And on some days, like today, she simply
needed to stay busy. It was her birthday, and although
Heath was taking her out tonight, it was still going to
be a difficult day. Lucas had always gone the extra
yard for her birthday.

When she'd first started working on this little cottage, it was a way to keep herself busy while she
mourned Lucas's death. She'd needed something
truly immersive, and it had to be physical. There
was a lot of cathartic release to be had from smash-
ing down walls with a sledgehammer and ripping up
floorboards with a crowbar. Of course, she'd been
sobbing through a lot of it, an actual sea of tears.
She'd never known it was possible to cry so much.
She kept waiting for the day when her grief would
finally dry up and go away. But that was the biggest lesson she had waiting for her—it didn't work
like that. The struggle didn't travel a straight line. It
was a roller coaster. A string of good days would be
followed by an unexpected descent back into sadness. Then the sun would come up and she'd heal
for a few days. Maybe a few weeks. Then the cycle
would start again.

Sometimes it was prompted by a memory, like of planning her wedding with Lucas. She'd thought her whole life was ahead of her then. She'd had no idea it was about to feel like it had come to an end. Right after Lucas was gone, she used to sleep with one of his shirts and the wedding planner notebook she'd been using to stay organized. A few months in, she'd realized how much she was torturing herself, and so she'd tucked away the notebook in the buffet. And she made the shirt into a pillow, but she put it on the bed in the guest room. It was a comfort to know that it was there if she needed it.

She kept an eye on the clock as she swept up the mess from the drywall and readied herself to start cutting two-by-fours for the framing. She was supposed to be at Heath's at five o'clock. Their dinner reservations for Sheen were at seven. He was adorable for having remembered that she'd mentioned it the first time he'd come to her house. He was even more adorable for insisting he take her out. He really was a generous person, and she couldn't see why others didn't see that in him. Maybe it was because he was so good at hiding it. He definitely wouldn't go out of his way to take or receive credit for anything. She had to admire that. Most people had too big an ego to not get every bit of credit they felt they deserved. But not Heath. People were free to take him or leave him. He didn't seem to care too much either way.

Around three thirty, she decided she'd better knock off for the day and hop in the shower. But before she could do that, her phone rang with a call from Heath. "Hey," she said. "I was just thinking about you. What's up?"

"I have a huge problem."

Ruby's stomach sank. She really hoped this didn't have anything to do with the Grandin or Lattimore families. "What's going on?"

"One of the horses got out of the barn, and I let my ranch hands leave early so they could go to an NBA game in Dallas. Normally, I'd wait for Lucky to come back. The whole property is fenced. But it's going to be dark soon and this horse is old, and she can't spend the night out in the cold."

"I was just about to get ready for our date. Do you want me to come over now and help you look?"

"I hate asking. I hate that this happened at all. It's your birthday and this is not how I wanted to spend it."

"I know that. It was your idea to celebrate at all. I'll come over now. But fair warning—I look like a wreck. No makeup, my hair is in a ponytail, and I probably smell pretty bad, too."

"I'm sure that, however you look, you're perfect."

"Famous last words, mister." She glanced at the gaping hole in the wall and decided that she'd have to clean up later. If she had any hope of salvaging her birthday date, she needed to help Heath now.

"Bring whatever you were going to wear tonight. If we find Lucky in time, we can still make it to Sheen. Or I'll call over there and ask them to move our seating time."

"One problem at a time, okay? I'll be there as quick as I can." Ruby hung up and quickly packed a bag with her clothes for their date, plus some makeup and her hair dryer. Feeling optimistic, she added an outfit for tomorrow. Maybe he would want her to sleep over. Maybe she and Heath could spend the entire day together.

She grabbed her coat and rushed outside, then raced to Heath's ranch, doing her best to not break any traffic laws, although she did run a yellow light at what could have been considered the last second. When she pulled up to his house, he was standing next to his truck, which was on one of the access roads that wound through the property. His vehicle was already running. She could see the billowy puffs of exhaust in the cold.

She parked her car and left her things inside, jogging over to his truck. "I told you I look like a wreck."

He smiled wide and pulled her closer, pressing a soft kiss to her lips. "You're more gorgeous than the last time I saw you."

That had been only a few days ago, and she'd been freshly showered at the time, so she was positive that wasn't true. "You're a pretty good liar."

"Not really." He opened the passenger's-side door of his truck. "Let's go. It's getting darker."

"And colder." Ruby climbed inside, thankful that Heath had the heat blazing.

"I already made one pass with the truck and I can't find her anywhere. We might have to go out into some of the pastures on foot, so I brought some flashlights. I know some of Lucky's hiding spots."

"She must be a pretty special horse. What breed is she?"

Heath laughed as he put the engine in Reverse. He made a quick three-point turn, and then they were on their way. "Not sure. She was a rescue. She was Ashley's horse."

Now Ruby understood why this was so urgent, aside from the animal's age and the dropping temperatures outside—he couldn't allow his sister's horse to suffer at all. "We'll find her."

"The whole thing was so stupid. I got distracted when I was putting her back in the stable late this afternoon. Pretty sure I forgot to double-latch her stall." He kept his eyes trained on the terrain as the truck bounced over the rough road and the headlights shone on their path. "She's mischievous. She sometimes makes a break for it. It's so bad that I keep a breakaway halter on her all the time. She actually has a tag like a dog."

"You'd think she'd get one whiff of how cold it is and head right back inside."

Heath glanced over at Ruby. "Yeah. Well. She hasn't been the same since Ashley died. It's like she misses her, which I know probably sounds a little unhinged."

Ruby looked out the passenger's-side window, scanning the landscape. "No sign of her over here. If you've already done one pass in the truck, maybe we should just accept that we'll need to go on foot. You mentioned that she has hiding places. Should we check those?"

"That's probably the best way to do this. Unfortunately, the most likely spot is also the least accessible. Are you sure you're up for this?"

"I already look like hell, so yes."

"No, you don't. But I'm going to agree with you about this approach." Heath took a sharp right and started over a long series of rolling ridges. About ten minutes later, he slowed down and pulled off to the side, gravel rumbling under the tires. A wooded area was to the right, with a small stand of bare hardwood trees with evergreens mixed in. It had to be a quarter mile away, down an incline and into a small valley. "There's a watering hole down there. She loves it." He zipped up his coat. "I can check it out if you want to stay in the car."

Ruby had come this far. She wasn't about to let him go on his own. "I'd like to go with you."

"Are you sure?"

She nodded eagerly. "Never been so sure in all my life."

Heath and Ruby started down the hill. He led the way, wanting to be sure he was there to catch her if she tripped. The sun had nearly dipped beneath the horizon, the temperature was dropping, and he was filled with a mix of emotions—worry over Lucky, appreciation for Ruby and regret that this had happened in the first place. "I hate that you're spending part of your birthday doing this."

"Well, the first part of my day was spent tearing out drywall."

"Another house project?"

"Yeah. I'm expanding my closet."

Heath remembered what she'd told him when they were dancing at the Texas Cattleman's Club, about what had sent her on her home improvement journey—working through her grief. "I hope that doesn't mean you were having a hard day because it's your birthday. Milestones can hit hard when you've lost someone."

"Actually, today was a good day. Right now, it's just about finishing up the house. Having that sense of accomplishment."

Heath really hoped that was the case. Off in the

distance, he heard the distinct sound of a horse's whinny. "That's her. That's Lucky." He picked up the pace. "Come on. She's probably down by the water."

"I'm right behind you," Ruby said.

Eventually, the slope eased up and flattened out, and they were able to run. He knew exactly where they were going and led Ruby into the trees, where it was far colder than out in the wide-open spaces. Even these bare trees had sheltered the area from the warmth of the sun. "Lucky! Lucky!" he shouted, dodging rocks and trees.

"There she is!" Ruby, who was running alongside him now, pointed off to the left.

Heath stopped dead in his tracks, realizing that Lucky wasn't at the water. She was in the spot where Heath had scattered some of Ashley's ashes. What could have possibly drawn Lucky to that particular place? A well of emotion rose up inside of him and he had to close his eyes to keep it at bay. He wasn't about to break down in front of Ruby.

"Are you okay?" she asked, breathless.

"I'm fine." He opened his eyes and shook his head in disbelief.

"Heath. Get real. You're obviously not okay. I can see it on your face."

How did she see right through him? "It's just that Lucky is in the exact spot where I left some of Ashley's ashes." He started walking toward Lucky. Ruby was right at his side.

"This must be a special place."

"Ashley showed Nolan and me this hiding spot. After our dad passed away. When the three of us needed to get away and just goof off. The watering hole isn't very deep, so we'd swim in there sometimes. Bring food or sneak some beer and talk. About the future." Just saying that word out loud—*future*—made him realize exactly how much he'd clung to the idea of better days ahead when he was younger. It was the only thing that kept him going. All of that hope went away when his mom and Ashley had their accident. And now Ruby had given him a reminder of how powerful even a drop of optimism could be. He still had hope that the Grandin and Lattimore families would own up to their mistakes so they could all move on.

Lucky whinnied again, making it even easier to see her as the warm breath rose from her nose in the frigid air. She rubbed her head up against a tree fitfully.

"How amazing is it that she came here?" Ruby asked as they closed in on the beautiful animal, sable brown with tufts of white along her nose and on her belly and tail. Ruby didn't hesitate to go right up to Lucky, although she was gentle and careful with her approach. Lucky warmed to her immediately, nudging at her arm as Ruby caressed her head and shushed her when she whinnied again.

"After all this time. I don't understand," Heath

said, struggling to wrap his head around the idea that, on some level, Lucky knew that some of Ashley's ashes were here.

"Animals are amazing. They know things. They understand when we're in pain. They love just like we do." Ruby looked into Lucky's eyes, and they seemed to share a special moment. It was the exact sort of connection Ashley had had with horses. They trusted her, and she adored them.

It was Heath's turn to give Lucky a rub behind her ears. "Today was not really the day to remind me about Ashley, Lucky. I'm supposed to take Ruby out for her birthday. Now we're going to have to rush to get to dinner." He turned to Ruby. "I can ride her back to the stable if you want to take the truck. And I'll meet you there?"

"You can ride bareback?"

"That's how I learned. And she'll do fine with her halter on. We're not going to be running at top speed."

"You need some serious core strength to stay up on a horse like that. Although, I've seen your abs, so I suppose it makes sense." Ruby laughed. "You amaze me."

You amaze me. Heath had pretty well ruined her birthday plans and Ruby was being nothing less than a very good sport about it. "I can hoist myself up there if I get on that rock." Ahead was a sizable boulder, probably three or four feet high. It would be just enough of a boost. He led Lucky over with her bridle, and sure enough, it gave him just the right angle to swing his leg over and mount the horse. "The keys are in the truck. Will you be okay?" he asked, looking down at Ruby.

"Yes. I'm going to drive slow, though, so I can keep an eye on you two."

"Probably a good idea."

Heath did his best to urge Lucky along, but she was showing her age and it was slow going. It took nearly twice as long to get back to the stable as it had with the truck. Every step of that ride gave Heath another minute to think about where he was in life and the women who had been so important to him. First Ashley and his mom, but now Ruby. In very short order, she had become an integral part of the puzzle that was his existence. She understood him on a level that very few people did, and she appreciated the losses he had endured. He hoped that when and if his push against the Grandin and Lattimore families came to light, she would know he had only done it out of love. During their lunch at the Royal Diner, she'd urged him to do what he needed to do to put it all to rest. Well, that was exactly what he'd set in motion.

Heath got Lucky settled back in her stall in the stable, which was toasty warm and comfortable. Surely the horse realized now that this was a far better place to be than out on the ranch, with no refuge from the cold. "Thank you for coming out," he said to Ruby, looking at his watch. "We have about a half hour until our reservation. We can hurry up and try to get ready, or I can call the restaurant and ask them to move our time. What do you think?"

Ruby shook her head. "You know, I don't really feel like going out at this point. I'd rather stay here. With you."

"Really? I feel like I've ruined your birthday."

"This is exactly my speed, to be honest."

He pulled her closer, wrapping his arms around her waist. He was so relieved that she didn't want to go to Sheen. Running into a Grandin and Lattimore and having them yell at him in the middle of a crowded restaurant would really ruin her birthday. Of course, he wasn't about to share his worries. That was his burden to bear. "That's what I like about you. Aside from the part where we froze our butts off finding a lost horse, this is my speed, too. Do you want to go back to the house so I can show you something?" he asked.

She smiled, the corner of her mouth quirking up adorably. "Is it something of yours? Because I've seen it all, but I wouldn't mind looking again."

He laughed and planted a kiss on her lips. "I love that your brain immediately turns to sex, but I'm actually talking about something else."

"Lead the way."

Heath and Ruby hopped in his truck and were back at the house in a few short minutes. Inside, he led her to his home office, which was right off the living room. "I just got the preliminary drawings for the riding center. No one else has seen them. I texted Nolan about it, but he hasn't gotten back to me." Just then, Heath's phone beeped with a text. "Speak of the devil," he said as he consulted the screen. "He wants to know if we'll have dinner with Chelsea and him at their place. I can bring the plans over then."

It sounded like a fabulous evening to Ruby, but she did worry that things were moving fast. She and Heath were spending so much time together. *Take a breath. You like him. It's okay to like him.* "That's sweet. Yes. I'd love to go."

Heath tapped away on his phone, then looked at her. "Friday okay?"

"That should work."

Heath finished one more text, then set his phone down and unfurled the first set of plans. "This is all very early. Just a few elevations to give me a sense of the direction for the project."

Ruby stood closer to him, peering down at the scroll of architectural drawings. "What's that?" she asked, pointing to a large building. When she'd been thinking "riding center," she'd only considered the corrals.

"That will be the main building, for administrative duties, a small visitors' center and classrooms." He peeled back a page to show a sketch of the rest of the center. "There will be three corrals. One fully enclosed, with seating for a crowd if we choose to do any shows. One will be open-air and the last one will be covered."

"This is a serious undertaking. How are you going to pay for all of this?"

"I have the money myself. But I'm working on some local contributions. I'd like the community to be invested in it." He turned to her and the soft lighting in his office lit him from the side, making him even more handsome. Or maybe it was the way this subject matter made him light up from within.

"I think that's a wonderful idea. You should do everything you can to make sure it's an integral part of Royal."

He put his arm around her shoulders and snuggled her closer, then planted a kiss on top of her head. "I love the way you think. You're always looking for ways to make things better. Which is ironic since you do that all on your own."

She turned to face him and they naturally drew each other into an embrace, one where they could still look at each other. "I'm not sure what that means."

"It means that you are an actual ray of sunshine, Ruby. You shine a light on things, good or bad, and try to figure out a way to make everything better." He cupped both sides of her face with his hands and peered into her eyes. From anyone else, this gesture might make her feel entirely too vulnerable. But his touch always made her feel safe. Protected. Adored.

"Do you know what I like so much about you, Heath?"

He grinned as he rubbed her cheek with his thumb. "Is this a trick question?"

She laughed quietly. "No. I'm trying to pay you a compliment. You're always saying nice things about me. You need to let me take a turn."

"Okay. Go for it."

"I like that you think about and consider everything. You have this rugged handsome exterior, but you are a very cerebral guy. It's very sexy."

"So you're saying I'm handsome..." He lowered his head to go in for a kiss.

She tugged him closer and raised her chin. "What I'm saying is that you're the whole package." He kissed her and all she wanted was to melt into him. She definitely wanted to rip off his clothes and spend the entire night going to town on each other. When he reached down and palmed her thigh, then hitched it up, she knew that was exactly where this was going. She broke free from the kiss. "Heath, I'm a wreck. I'd like to clean up before things go any further."

"Me too. I think we can kill two birds with one stone and have a whole lot of fun while we do it. Come on." He grabbed her hand and led her through his bedroom, into his luxurious bathroom. There was masculine slate tile and a long vanity topped with Carrara marble. The glass shower enclosure was built for two. Absolutely perfect.

Heath wasted zero time turning on the water in the shower while Ruby pulled out her ponytail and removed the small gold stud earrings she was wearing. He pulled off his boots and stripped off the rest of his clothes in record time. Her breath hitched when she saw how hard he was already. She wasn't sure what she'd done to be so lucky. Heath turned his attention to her, pushing her sweater up over her head. She loved the way he looked at her, the way his eyes got stormy and dark with each new item of clothing removed. Her boots and socks, jeans and bra, and finally, her panties. Standing there, completely naked, she had every reason to feel too exposed. Too vulnerable. But she felt nothing but turned on, which was a feat in its own right since he'd hardly touched her.

He opened the shower door and she stepped into the warm spray, her muscles immediately relaxing. Heath joined her and closed the door, then positioned himself behind her. He pressed his erection against her bottom and placed his hands on her hips, caressing them as he kissed her neck. His touch was soft and sensuous, all while the steam rose around them. "Your skin is so damn soft, Ruby. I could touch you forever."

Forever. In her recent history, that was a word that had become meaningless. Then she'd met Heath and things started to change. "I love having your hands all over me."

He reached past her for a bar of soap and rolled

it in his hands, his arms threaded under hers. He spread the creamy lather up her stomach, then over her breasts, his hands slowly working in circles, rubbing her nipples with the palms of his hands. Ruby reached above her head and clasped her hands back behind his neck, giving him complete access to every inch of her torso. She pressed her bottom harder against his steely length, wagging her hips back and forth. Heath groaned his approval into her neck, then rinsed off one of his hands. He caressed her belly, then slid his fingers lower, spreading her delicate folds until he found her center. He rubbed in languid circles while he cupped one of her breasts with his other hand. The pressure was building so fast in her body it was hard to think straight, especially as the hot water streamed down her thighs. Heath started to move faster. Harder. And that made the tension tighter, winding and winding, completing a circuit between her clit and her nipple, until finally it all peaked. She knocked her head back against Heath's shoulder and cried out.

He slowed his hand between her legs, then turned her in his arms. She kissed him deeply as the waves of pleasure were still rolling over her. "That was amazing."

"Think of it as the first course."

"I don't care how good the food is at Sheen, it's definitely not *that* good."

Heath chuckled. "Let me get cleaned up and we can see exactly how good it can get around here."

Ruby grabbed the bar of soap and spread silky bubbles across his firm chest while he worked shampoo through his hair. Even after that dizzying orgasm, she still hadn't had enough of him. She needed everything. He rinsed off the soap, then turned off the water. As they stepped out of the shower, the bathroom felt just as warm, so they didn't bother with towels and instead wrapped up in each other's arms. Their slick wet skin rubbed together as he walked her backward to the vanity.

Ruby reached back for the counter, but Heath went one better, cupped her butt in his hands and lifted her. The cool stone counter made her arch her back, which only left her closer to him. She coiled her legs around his waist, dug her hands into his wet hair, kissing him as their tongues wound together and water went everywhere. "Condom?" she had the presence of mind to ask.

"Yes. Right here." He opened a cabinet and pulled out a small box, then rolled the condom onto himself. He wasted no time, grabbing her hips and pulling her to the edge of the counter, then guiding himself inside. Their gazes connected while he did it, and the intensity of that moment overwhelmed her. There was nothing else in the world other than Heath at that moment. His first strokes were slow and deep, and she dug her heels into his ass, wanting him even closer.

She could tell from his breaths and facial expressions that he was already close. His eyes kept drifting shut and his lips were slack. She pushed against him harder with the motion of her hips. She didn't want him to be gentle, caring Heath. She wanted him to unleash whatever it was that drove him to do some of the things he did. The things people hated him for. He read her intent and drove into her faster, sending her barreling toward her second peak. She leaned back and flattened her hands on the vanity, if only to counter the force of his thrusts. She smiled when she noticed how he was momentarily hypnotized by the bounce of her breasts.

Ruby was so close to the brink that she could taste it. She could *see* it. And then, finally, with one more stroke, her torso jerked forward and Heath followed, his breaths choppy and torn as he pulled her chest to his and they rode out the waves together. All that was left was quiet, warmth, and the *thump thump thump* as his heartbeat matched hers. They were in sync. Blissfully so. And she knew then that she had fallen right off the cliff and into the waiting arms of Heath.

Nine

With every passing day, Ruby was growing closer to Heath. She was getting in a little deeper. At her strongest moments, when she was in his arms and the sun was shining and she saw the promise of a new day, it felt wonderful. It felt right. He was not only a surprise in her life, he was a gift. He made her remember how amazing it was to laugh with someone, so hard that your legs went weak and your stomach hurt. He reminded her how incredible it was to glance at another person, lock eyes and have an entire conversation without a single word exchanged. Those moments almost always ignited the passion between them. Time and place ceased to mean a thing. All that existed for Ruby was Heath and she wanted to think he felt the same way.

But there were times, usually in the middle of the night when she couldn't sleep, that her feelings scared the hell out of her. It had hurt so much to lose Lucas. It changed her forever. Was she really ready to be all in with Heath? She truly wanted to be, but she shuddered to think how badly it would destroy her if things didn't work out. That would feel like it had before. Like she was having her heart ripped out. She couldn't live through that again. It almost killed her the first time.

Her biggest concern when she'd first met Heath had been his crusade against the Grandins and the Lattimores. She could not be with a man who was living a life that kept him looking backward, or at the very least always looking over his shoulder. Her only path was forward. It had taken her three years to figure that out. It was only after months and months of desperately longing for what had been that she'd learned that some things were gone forever. And there was nothing anyone could do about it. Some things simply had to be let go, with a reluctant uncurling of fingers as you allowed that person or vexing situation to simply slip away. It didn't mean that you didn't care. It didn't mean that your love for someone wasn't strong. It meant that your strength and energy needed to go into living.

Thankfully, Heath hadn't brought up his dispute with the families since their night at the TCC, or if he did, it was only to crack a joke or make a dismissive comment under his breath, something that could be quickly cast aside. Ever since the day they'd run into each other in downtown Royal at the Rancher's Daughter and they had lunch at the diner, her approach had been to keep him focused on Ashley's foundation and the riding center. It genuinely excited him. It made him optimistic and enthusiastic. That was the Heath Thurston she adored. That was the man she had fallen for.

Tonight, they were going to dinner at Chelsea and Nolan's apartment. In Ruby's mind, this was going to be a big test. She really wanted to see how he interacted with Chelsea in a more intimate setting. The only other time she'd been with them both had been New Year's Eve at the Texas Cattleman's Club. They'd been congenial toward each other, but that was easy in a crowded celebratory setting with champagne flowing.

"I didn't realize Nolan and Chelsea lived downtown," Ruby said as she and Heath walked hand in hand from the spot where Heath had parked the car.

"Yep. They have a pretty cool loft, but it's just a rental. They're planning on breaking ground on a house in the spring. Chelsea was gifted twenty acres of the Grandin property on her twenty-first birthday."

Ruby had to wonder if that was a hard pill for Heath to swallow. He'd spent so much time raging against the Grandin family, particularly about their property, and now his brother was going to go live on it? Plus, inheritance was at the core of what Heath had been pursuing all along. If Ashley was still alive and the Grandins had acknowledged her place in their family, she should have been given a similar birthday present. That couldn't be an easy fact for Heath to accept. "Building a house from the ground up sounds exciting."

"It is. They've got their whole lives ahead of them." Heath pointed ahead to a door near the corner. "This is it." He pressed a button for the intercom and moments later they were buzzed into the building.

"Building a house also sounds like a lot of work," Ruby added as they entered a stairwell and headed upstairs. "I can't imagine having to pick everything out. Tile, flooring, paint colors, appliances. It would be exhausting."

"So says the woman who redid her entire home. On her own. Most people would say that was impossible. I still can't believe you did that."

"It helped me move ahead. Just like you have the riding center and Ashley's foundation. It's basically the same thing."

"I suppose you're right. It's good to focus on something positive."

It warmed Ruby from head to toe to know that Heath was focusing on the good. It helped her believe that they could have a future together. A few weeks ago, that would have been a scary thought, but so much had happened since then. Every day was another step toward something more lasting.

When they arrived at Nolan's door, Heath gave it a knock, but never let go of Ruby's hand. Nolan was quick to answer with Chelsea at his side. They both erupted in an eager welcome, ushering Ruby and Heath inside.

"Oh, wow," Ruby said as she got her first glimpse of their apartment. As Heath had mentioned, it was a true loft, with an open space containing a living room area at its heart, an open kitchen on the far wall, and a bedroom area in one corner, complete with a king bed. It had a casual sophistication to it that Ruby really liked—a blending of comfort, color and style. "What a cool space. I love it."

"Thank you," Chelsea said. "We won't be here too much longer, but it works."

"Heath mentioned that you're about to break ground on the house you're building on your family's property. How exciting."

Chelsea and Nolan looked into each other's eyes with nothing less than pure adoration. "I can't wait," Nolan said. "We can't start a family living here. And we're really eager to get pregnant."

Heath cleared his throat. "Wow. I wasn't really expecting that bit of news." His voice wobbled with surprise.

"Are you surprised?" Nolan asked.

"I suppose I am," Heath answered. "It wasn't that

long ago that you were the guy running all over the world. It's a big change."

Nolan eyed Heath. "Love has changed me. Chelsea has changed me. I don't need the things I used to chase. All I care about is our relationship." He turned back to Chelsea. "All I need is you."

"That's so sweet, babe," Chelsea said. "Really. I love you so much."

"I love you, too," Nolan replied, then kissed her on the forehead.

Ruby felt as though her heart was going to pound right out of her chest and not in a good way. She couldn't read Heath's reaction at all and she worried that this might upset him. After all, his war had been waged against the Grandin family, and now his twin brother was not only married to a Grandin, he was ready to start having children with one.

"What are you thinking?" Nolan asked Heath.

"Honestly?" Heath let a breathy laugh escape his lips. "I'm happy. I love the thought of you and Chelsea becoming parents. I love the idea of being an uncle, and especially since you're going to stay in Royal, where I get to be a part of it. I never thought this day would come, Nolan."

Heath's voice was truly breaking with a mix of elation and raw emotion. He reached for his brother and the two embraced. Ruby looked over at Chelsea through watery eyes, noticing that Chelsea was crying, too. It was then that Ruby realized exactly how much of Heath's crusade had been about nothing more than needing the love of family. Who could possibly fault him for that? Surely not Ruby. She needed it, too.

"You two are going to ruin my mascara," Chelsea said, wiping the tears away.

Nolan and Heath stepped out of their hug, but held strong eye contact for a few moments. It was a powerful image—two identical men having a conversation only they could have, without words. "I love you," Heath said. "I'm so glad you're back in my life."

"It's good to be back. I love you, too," Nolan replied.

Ruby hadn't realized until right then that she'd been holding her breath. How could so much healing possibly be packed into such a short amount of time? She wasn't sure, but she was thankful she'd been there to see it.

"Okay, then." Nolan looked at Ruby and smiled, then turned back to Chelsea. "I think we could all use a glass of wine."

"Great idea. Dinner will be ready in a few minutes, and then we can sit down and talk and eat and enjoy," Chelsea said.

"Did you bring the riding center plans?" Nolan asked Heath.

"I didn't. The second round is almost ready. I

didn't want to show you plans that would change in a few days."

"Okay. Let's get together when you have them," Nolan replied.

Chelsea turned to Ruby. "Want to help me get the last few things ready?"

"Absolutely." Ruby followed Chelsea into the kitchen while Heath and Nolan wandered over to a tall wine rack in the corner of the apartment.

"Do you want to go ahead and toss the salad?" Chelsea asked. "Everything's ready to go in that big bowl on the island and the dressing is in the fridge door."

"Sure thing." Ruby followed Chelsea's directive. "That was pretty intense," she said as she removed the top from the dressing and lightly drizzled it on the greens.

"It was. But it's been a long time coming. They've been getting closer since Nolan returned to Royal, but some scars run pretty deep. I'm not entirely sure either of them truly trusted each other. I think it has helped that Heath seems to have dropped his crusade against my family and that Nolan is going to help with Ashley's foundation."

Ruby tossed the salad, feeling fortunate that she'd witnessed that momentous exchange between the brothers. It was one more positive note in the case she was making for herself, one that said she and Heath Thurston belonged together.

* * *

Dinner was amazing, even though Chelsea hadn't prepared it. She admitted that she wasn't much of a cook, but she'd ordered a heat-and-eat meal from a local chef that included a hearty pasta dish with braised pork, tomato, fresh herbs and lots of Parmesan. It was flat-out delicious. Even so, the real highlight was the four of them at that tiny dining table, talking, laughing, eating, and drinking wine. There was no negativity or acrimony, only genuine affection and good feelings. They were making memories, and for the first time in a long time, they were happy ones.

Heath had never imagined such a scene would be possible with a member of the Grandin family, but clearly it was. He was also now convinced that his brother had absolutely made the right decision in marrying Chelsea. They were perfect for each other, which made Heath realize that there was another perfect fit in the room—he and Ruby. How had she so effortlessly folded herself into his life? How had they become so impossibly close in such a short amount of time? He wasn't sure of any of the answers. He only knew that he considered himself lucky. Very, very lucky.

After dinner, Heath and Nolan volunteered for cleanup duty while Chelsea and Ruby hung out in the living room and talked about decor choices for Nolan and Chelsea's new house.

"Fatherhood. It's a big step," Heath said to Nolan, taking a clean plate from him to dry. "I'm proud of you."

Nolan glanced at him and smiled. "Thanks. I guess it just feels like the most natural thing in the world. And that's something I never imagined myself saying."

Heath laughed and put away the dish, then took another. "You know who would be really happy about this?"

"Ashley?" Nolan asked.

"Yes. Exactly."

Stillness settled over them for a moment. "She would have made such an amazing aunt. And Mom always had her troubles dealing with us, but I'm sure she would have been a proud grandmother."

"Oh, God. Yes. They absolutely would have loved it." Heath was surprised to realize that although the sadness over their mother's and sister's untimely deaths might never go away, he could actually talk about them now without getting angry or upset.

"It's okay. They're going to get the best uncle in the world."

Heath laughed, but he had to think about that for a moment. Would the best uncle in the world ever threaten to sue his sister-in-law's family? No. Nothing had come of the letter Albert had sent other than an eventual response from Victor Grandin Jr. and Ben Lattimore, which asked for more time, but it was still out there in the world, like a land mine. How long before someone, probably him, would step on it? It was probably time to put it all to an end. Everything tonight had been so wonderful. Why would he want to ruin everything that was ahead for the four people in this room? He didn't want to do that. He didn't even want to risk it.

"Thanks a ton for inviting us over tonight. This was so much fun. Ruby and I have both had a great time," Heath said.

"Hold on a second. Let me go grab my phone so I can record you saying that you had fun." Nolan's devilish grin said that he was joking around, but Heath was still a little hurt by it.

"Hey. I like to have fun as much as the next person."

Nolan nodded and looked across the room. "You've definitely been inching toward that since you met Ruby. Which is part of the reason we invited you two over tonight. Chelsea and I will do anything to encourage this relationship."

"She's pretty amazing, isn't she?"

Nolan looked back at Heath and shook his head. "Yes. She is. But it's not just her. It's the two of you together. Heath, you have so much good inside of you and it's been hidden away. I'm really glad to see it all come back out. I look at you and see the brother I used to know."

"I can admit that I do feel more like my old self. I got lost there for a pretty long time."

"It's not surprising. Mom's and Ashley's deaths were a shock to us both. It was horrible. But…" Nolan stared down at the floor, seeming weighed down by something.

"But what?"

He raised his head and made eye contact with Heath. "I hate to say this."

"Whatever it is, come out with it. You can tell me anything and everything."

"Of course I'm heartbroken over the accident. I always will be. But I have to wonder what would have happened between you and me if that hadn't happened. What if they were still here? How would things be different?"

Heath had pondered this scenario a million times. He'd thought about what would have happened if they'd left the house five minutes earlier or five minutes later. It was the cruel twist of fate that really ate at him. "You and I wouldn't be having this conversation. I know that much. Our relationship would still be strained. Or nonexistent. Which is probably more accurate."

"Right. Exactly. Now, the old me would have seen the whole situation in black and white, but Chelsea has helped me see the shades of gray. Losing Mom and Ashley was terrible, but it brought us back together. We're all going to die someday. That was their day. And as tragic as that was, good still came out of it."

"I never really looked at it that way." Nolan had just blown Heath's mind. It might take him a long time to wrap his head around the concept.

"Anyway. That's one of those things that popped into my head in the middle of the night when I couldn't sleep because I was worried about you. About us."

"I've had those same sleepless nights." Too many to count.

"I bet you have."

"I don't want either of us to have those anymore, Nolan. We're moving forward, okay? You and I, together, as brothers."

"That is music to my ears."

"Hey, Nolan," Chelsea said. "Can you come over here and explain to Ruby that thing you want to do with the flooring in the kitchen? I still don't really understand it."

"Sure thing." Nolan glanced at Heath. "Do you want to come and see?"

"Actually, I need to send a text real quick. I'll be over in a minute." Heath watched as his brother crossed the room. Then he turned his back to them, pulled out his phone and tapped out a quick text to Albert. *Changed my mind. Tell them there will be no lawsuit. Whatever you need to do.* It felt like an eternity passed as he stared at his phone, waiting to hear back from Albert. Eventually, a few moments later, he got a reply.

You sure?

Heath had to smile at the question. He'd never been more sure of anything in his life. Yes. Kill it.

Right away.

"Everything okay?" Ruby asked, coming up behind him and placing her hands on his shoulders.

He turned and pulled her into his arms. "Everything's perfect."

She rested her chin on his chest and peered up at him. "Want to get out of here?"

His body responded with a wave of warmth that only Ruby could bring about. It was amazing that she had that sort of effect on him. "I do. Are you and Chelsea all done?"

"Yep. And guess what? Chelsea and I made a date to go shopping together at the Rancher's Daughter next weekend. Morgan will have all of the new spring clothes then."

"That sounds like fun."

"So maybe you and Nolan can get together to talk about the riding center then."

"That should be perfect. I should have the full plans by then." He took her hand and they walked over to Chelsea and Nolan in the living room area, where they were seated on the couch, looking over their house plans. "Hey, Nolan. Ruby and I are going to head out. Do you want to go over the riding center plans next week when Chelsea and Ruby are shopping?"

"Sounds good," Nolan said as he and Chelsea got up from the couch and made their way to the front door. "I'll talk to you soon?" he asked Heath.

Heath loved that everything was coming together so well. The woman he was head over heels for had already become close with his brother, the person he cared about most in the world. And as for Chelsea, Heath's opinion of her had softened considerably. Seeing her interact with Ruby so effortlessly certainly helped. "Yes. And thanks again to you both for dinner. It was an amazing night. I hope we can do it again."

Nolan opened the door for Ruby and Heath. "I'm counting on it."

Ten

Ruby was excited by the prospect of her shopping trip with Chelsea, and not just because Heath had given her his credit card and instructed her to buy whatever she wanted. Chelsea had quickly become a good friend, which really helped Ruby feel more connected to Royal. Before she met Heath, she'd felt like a stranger in this small town, but as he introduced her to the people in his life, her social circle was widening, and she realized how much she'd cut herself off from everything and everyone after Lucas died. It was nice to be a part of something once again, and Chelsea was definitely a big piece in that puzzle.

"Are you sure you want to pay?" Ruby asked Heath as they stood outside of the Rancher's Daughter, waiting for Chelsea and Nolan to meet them. It was a chilly morning, and she and Heath had their arms wrapped around each other, although, to be fair, that was the case most of the time.

"I'm positive," Heath said. "Buy whatever you want. I don't care how much it costs."

"I have my own money, you know."

"I'm aware of that. But your birthday wasn't everything I wanted it to be. So let me do this one nice thing for you, okay?"

Ruby peered up at him, admiring his handsome face and also getting warm and fuzzy feelings about his generous nature. "You do nice things for me all the time. You were more than nice to me last night." Ruby had been staying over at Heath's all week long. Every night was an exploration of the heat and passion between them, but Heath had really outdone himself a mere twelve hours ago. Just thinking about it sent a thrill along her spine.

"Hey. I enjoyed it, too. Trust me."

"Jeez, you two. Get a room." Nolan's voice came out of nowhere, making Ruby jump. He placed his hands on her shoulders, giving her a gentle squeeze.

"Good morning to you, too," Heath said.

"Hey, guys," Chelsea chimed in as she appeared and patted Heath on the arm before directing her attention to Ruby. "Are we ready to do some serious damage in my sister's store?"

Ruby grinned. "Absolutely." She slid Heath a look of reassurance. "Well, not too much damage."

"You guys are going to go grab a late breakfast at the diner?" Chelsea asked.

Heath nodded eagerly, holding up the cardboard tube that contained the architect's plans. "Yes. I've got the drawings and the preliminary budget for the riding center. I want to go over all of that with Nolan, and we'll talk about funding the endowment."

"I'd love to volunteer when it's up and running."

"Thank you." Heath leaned closer to Ruby and kissed her. "Have fun."

"I will."

Chelsea and Nolan gave each other a quick kiss. "I love you," Chelsea said.

"Love you, too," Nolan replied.

The exchange between Chelsea and Nolan played in her head, and Ruby realized the one thing missing from her otherwise perfect relationship with Heath were those three little words. She looked at him and their gazes connected, but she could only imagine how odd she must look because Heath seemed puzzled. If only he knew the confusion between her head and heart. Was she really ready to tell Heath that she loved him? The idea felt surprisingly natural. What a revelation that was. When they'd met, she couldn't have imagined she'd ever say it again to anyone.

"See you guys in a little bit," Chelsea said, opening the door to the shop.

Ruby followed Chelsea inside, still a little dazed by her realization that she was ready to tell Heath she loved him. It had come hard and fast like a bolt of lightning during a summer thunderstorm, although she supposed she should have seen it coming.

Morgan looked up from her spot behind the register and rushed out to greet them. "I'm so excited for you two to see all of the new stuff. I pulled a bunch of things for you both to look at. It's all back by the dressing rooms."

Chelsea and Ruby followed, and sure enough, there was a vast array of cute warm-weather clothes waiting for them on a rolling rack. There were summery dresses, adorable sleeveless tops, several different types of skirts, and Ruby's favorite, blue jeans. Just seeing the clothes made her excited for summer. She was officially *over* winter.

"I guess we'd better get to trying some of this stuff on, huh?" Chelsea asked.

"Get your butts in there," Morgan said. "I've put enough stuff for you both to get started in the dressing rooms. Ruby, you're on the right. Chelsea, you're the left."

"I can't wait to see what you picked out," Chelsea said.

"It's a lot more fun now that you've expanded beyond blue jeans," Morgan replied with a laugh.

Ruby and Chelsea took their respective rooms.

Ruby zipped the curtain closed and put down her purse, then pulled off her sweater to try on the first top.

"Let me know if any of the sizes are off," Morgan called. "I'll be sitting here, checking my email."

Ruby was turning in the mirror to admire this first item of clothing, a gauzy sleeveless black blouse with lace trim, when she heard Morgan's voice shrieking with panic.

"Oh, my God. Chelsea. Get out here. Right now."

"What's wrong?" Chelsea asked with a similarly frantic tone.

"Are you even listening to me? Please. Get out here. Now."

Ruby ducked out of her dressing room to see what was going on. Chelsea was a step ahead of her.

"Look at this." Morgan thrust her phone in her sister's face.

"What is it?" Chelsea asked.

"The county attorney just announced his reelection campaign. And at the same time, he announced an investigation and pending charges against our family and the Lattimores. He's saying that he believes both families have committed fraud. He used the word *conspiracy.*"

Chelsea took the phone, and although Ruby was scared to look, she stepped closer to see what all of the fuss was about. She instantly recognized the design of the local newspaper's website. There on the screen was a still image of an important-looking man named Nelson Redfield. The story was beneath it. Chelsea began scrolling, shaking her head. A few paragraphs in, Chelsea looked up at Morgan. "It says he was tipped off by *private* legal actions against the families, brought forth by another member of the Royal community. And it specifically mentions oil rights."

Ruby's mind immediately went to one person— Heath. Her stomach sank to her feet. "You don't think it could be…"

"It has to be Heath. Who else could it be?" Chelsea's voice was spilling over with distress. "Nolan worried that he'd do something like this. We need to go talk to both of them. Right now."

"I'm calling Vic. Maybe he knows what this means." Morgan took her phone from her sister and stalked back toward the register.

Chelsea rushed back into her dressing room, presumably to change her clothes, leaving Ruby standing there in shock. Her first instinct was to run down the street to find Heath and warn him that the Grandins, or at least Chelsea and possibly Morgan, were ready to blame him for all of this. There had to be another explanation.

Just as she was about to return to the dressing room, she caught sight of Nolan and Heath charging into the store. Nolan was leading the way, with Heath close on his heels.

"Where's Chelsea?" Nolan asked Ruby. All color had drained from his face.

"I'm here," Chelsea answered, bursting out of the fitting room. She flew past Nolan and headed straight for Heath. "What in the hell did you do?"

Heath froze. "I'm as confused as you are. I don't know how Nelson Redfield would have found out about anything I did. It was all between me and my lawyer."

Ruby rushed to Heath's side. "Between you and your lawyer? You were still pursuing legal action? I thought you decided not to do that."

"He's talking *criminal* charges, Heath," Chelsea blurted. "That means a trial. That means members of my family in jail. We could lose everything. And they're talking about it in the damn newspaper. Our reputations could be completely ruined."

Nolan placed his hands on his wife's shoulders. It partly looked like he wanted to calm her down. It partly looked like he needed to hold her back. "Hold on a second. Let's take a deep breath and talk this through. We don't need to start worrying about worst-case scenarios right away. A whole lot would need to happen before that. There has to be a way out of this."

"Just so everyone knows, I instructed my lawyer to drop the whole thing," Heath said. "All of it. So I don't see how I'm at fault here."

"But when, Heath? What was the timing?" Ruby's

mind was racing, running through the chronology of their relationship. That first day they'd met, he'd gotten angry when he understood the timing of the first survey. But by the next day, he'd seemed ready to move on. Although there had been plenty of times he got upset about the Grandin and Lattimore families, he'd backed down every time. Ruby had assumed he was moving on. Moving *forward*. So that they could do that together.

Morgan strode over from the checkout counter and looked straight at her sister. "I just got off the phone with Vic. Mom and Dad were sent a threatening letter by Heath's lawyer on December 30. They didn't tell us because they were trying to keep it quiet until they figured out their next steps." Morgan turned and delivered a death stare to Heath. "They were waiting to see if you might change your mind."

"I *did* change my mind," Heath pleaded. "Why does no one understand that?"

"Hold on a minute," Nolan interjected and faced Heath. "December 30? You and I and Chelsea and Ruby went to the TCC together the next night. We had you over for dinner a week ago. And all that time, you were being nice to my wife's face while you were going after her family? What kind of sick person does that? And when in the hell are you going to finally let this go?"

Ruby saw the moment when Heath was deflated by his brother's words. She could see the conflict buried deep inside him bubbling to the surface. He'd talked a big game about letting go, but he couldn't. The memories of Ashley and his mother were that strong. His need to get justice for them was so powerful that it made him do things he was now ashamed of.

"Heath Thurston, you just won't rest until you destroy my family, will you?" Chelsea asked.

"And I suppose it's perfectly okay that your family destroyed mine," he snapped back at Chelsea. He then turned to Nolan. "*Our* family."

Nolan shook his head. "We have been through this and I've been extremely clear about it. If you make me pick a side, I'm picking Chelsea's. She's my wife, Heath. She's my whole life."

Ruby felt like her heart was being torn in ten different directions. She felt bad for everyone, but she couldn't ignore the other feeling that wouldn't go away. Heath wasn't the man she'd thought he was. All she could do was look back at their time together and realize that every moment she'd thought she was falling in love with him, he wasn't being truthful. What sort of future could they possibly have together under those circumstances?

"Chelsea and I are going." Nolan turned to Heath. "Fix this or I will never forgive you. And just so you know, there's still a good chance I will never forgive you."

Chelsea didn't even say a thing. She stormed back

to the dressing room, grabbed her purse, kissed Morgan on the cheek, then walked right out of the store with Nolan at her side.

Heath watched as Chelsea and Nolan walked out of the Rancher's Daughter. *What a mess. What an absolute mess.* He turned to Ruby, needing her touch. Her reassurance. Her confidence in him. "This is not what I wanted to have happen. This was all an accident. A misunderstanding."

"Heath, the thing I'm struggling with right now is the timeline. I feel more than a little betrayed. I...I...I feel like you lied to me."

"Hey, you two." Morgan's tone was biting. "You're going to need to have your lovers' quarrel somewhere else. I'd like to close early for the day so I can go console my parents, who are now completely beside themselves."

Heath had felt plenty bad over the course of his life, but this was a new low—getting kicked out of a clothing boutique in the middle of downtown Royal. "Do you need help getting your things?" he asked Ruby.

"No. I got it. I need to change." She walked off for the fitting room, leaving only Heath and Morgan and the world's most uncomfortable silence.

"I'm going to fix this," he said to Morgan.

"Uh-huh. Right." Her voice dripped with sarcasm.

"Okay. I get it. You have zero confidence in me, but I am going to fix it."

"Let me put it this way. Your words don't mean a whole lot right now. Okay?" Morgan jangled her keys impatiently in her hand.

Of course, Heath had no earthly clue how he was going to fix this. He had no connections with Nelson Redfield, and how in the hell did you go about getting criminal charges dropped? Funnily enough, this news would have made him ecstatic six months ago. He would have been dancing in the streets. Now? He felt nothing less than utter devastation. He'd hurt the people he cared about most in this world, including his brother, just as they'd finally gotten back to a good place with their relationship. Heath might never forget the look on his brother's face when they'd been sitting down to breakfast, and the diner became abuzz with the news story. But even worse than that was the situation with Ruby. She'd used the word *betrayed*. How was he supposed to come back from that?

Ruby emerged from the dressing room, looking dejected. "I'm so sorry, Morgan. I'll come back to shop later."

"That sounds great. I look forward to seeing you. But please tell your boyfriend to stay at home next time. He's no longer welcome in my store."

Heath felt the anger rise up inside him. He had to rush to Ruby's defense, even when he knew that it would be far more advantageous if he held his head up and walked right out of the shop. "Morgan, please don't take it out on Ruby. She hasn't done a single thing to deserve it. You're welcome to be as mean as you want to me."

"I'll take that under advisement," Morgan said.

Ruby walked past Heath, shaking her head. "Please don't make it worse," she said under her breath, then kept going right on through the door.

Heath closed his eyes and pinched the bridge of his nose, then followed her outside. "Ruby. Please," he called after her. "Let me explain."

She was already nearly fifty yards ahead of him, taking hurried strides toward his truck. She didn't respond to his plea. She didn't turn back. Heath was smart enough to know when a woman was angry with him. Hell, he'd just stood there and taken it from Chelsea and Morgan, and it had hurt. But seeing Ruby's anger and disappointment was an entirely different experience. It cut him to the core. And he was desperate to make it stop.

He ran to catch up, but she was already at the truck, standing at the passenger's door and avoiding eye contact. Heath clicked the fob and waited for Ruby to get in before he did the same. Part of him was worried she'd take off running the instant he climbed in and put on his seat belt. "Ruby, I'm so sorry that happened," he said once they were both inside. "It had to have been horribly embarrassing."

He reached for her arm, needing to touch her. It created an ache square in the center of his chest.

She stared down at his hand on her, then shook
her head and pulled her arm away, turning toward
the window. "Drive, Heath. Just take me back to your
place so I can get my car and go home."

Heath swallowed hard. "I think we should talk
about this."

"Just drive." Uncomfortable silence filled the
cabin of his truck like poisonous gas, making it hard
to breathe. Ruby turned to him and their gazes connected. Her eyes were ringed in pink and full of pain.
"Please drive, Heath. I'm begging you."

He didn't need any more persuading. Perhaps
she was right. They just needed to get to his place.
Cool off. Then they could figure out what to do next.
He started the truck and headed home. A million
thoughts tumbled through his mind. He had a lot
of things to fix right now, and although the most
logical place to start was with a long conversation
with Albert, he was far more concerned with mend-
ing things with Ruby. Surely she would understand
where he was coming from. She always had before.
It was part of what had drawn him to her. Why would
now be any different?

As he pulled into his driveway and headed up to
the house, he decided that he would let Ruby take
the lead on this. He'd done an excellent job digging
himself a hole with his words. He didn't need to be

in any deeper. He parked in front of the house and killed the engine, then opened his door, but Ruby didn't move. "Are you coming inside?"

She shook her head. "No. I'm going to leave in a minute. But I have a few things I need to say first, and I don't want to go back inside your house, and I don't want to stand outside and freeze to death."

Heath immediately closed his truck door. It wasn't worth arguing that they would be far more comfortable in his living room, sitting in front of a roaring fire with something strong to drink. "Of course. Whatever you want. Why don't you tell me what you're thinking? And don't hold back. Let it rip. I figure we might as well get it all out now."

She took several long breaths in through her nose and blew them out through her mouth, like she was trying to center herself. "You know what, Heath? I know that justice for your mother and sister means a lot to you." Her voice was already cracking with emotion, which made Heath's heart bind up into a tight ball. "But I had hoped that your better nature would win out. That you wouldn't break up another family's legacy just to fulfill your own."

"This isn't about *my* legacy. It's about my sister and everything she can't do because she's not here."

"Listen to what you just said. Ashley isn't here anymore. Neither is your mother. They're both gone. And I'm not sure you've come to terms with that. You can't get real justice for a memory. You can't.

Anything you accomplish with a lawsuit will be for you. No one else."

The hurt in her voice was like a knife to the center of his chest, but he accepted that he had to hear these things, even when he didn't fully agree. "I don't think that's entirely true. The foundation will help people. You've said it yourself. Plus, is it so wrong that it matters to me? I'm here. I'm not a memory. I'm sitting right here with you, Ruby. And I need you to understand where I was coming from when I made one last attempt at getting the Grandins and Lattimores to own up to their misdeeds."

"Do you think I don't understand that you're holding on to more than a memory?" she croaked. "I know the difference between someone being here and not being here. Every minute of my existence is wrapped around knowing the difference. I lived through that when I lost Lucas."

"And that's one of the reasons we grew so close so quickly. We have that shared experience. We are cut from the same cloth, Ruby."

"We are not the same. You have this need to get even. You're vindictive. And it's your vindictiveness that's gotten everyone into this situation. I thought I knew you, but clearly I do not."

At first Heath had no response to that. Ruby's words were still slicing through him. After a few weighty moments, he said, "I hope you realize that being vindictive is not a normal part of my personality. If I ever became that way, it was because of things others did. I didn't start this."

"And I'm so tired of hearing that story, Heath. At some point, you have to let it go."

"I did let it go. I have. I told my lawyer to drop the suit. I don't see why everyone doesn't understand that. I had no way of knowing Nelson Redfield would get wind of any of this. And if the Grandin and Lattimore families committed a crime, that's not my fault."

"That's not what I'm angry about. I'm angry because the whole time we've been together, we had dozens of talks about the importance of moving on. And now I know that you were just saying things that you didn't really mean. That whole time, you weren't actually moving on. How am I supposed to believe that anything between us was real? That it was anything more than sex?"

Heath could not believe what she was saying to him right now. Was her opinion of him really that poor? "You really don't believe that what happened between us was real? Do you have any idea how much that hurts me? I told you about my mom and my sister. I told you my deepest feelings about everything that happened to my family. That was all real to me. Just like it was real when you told me about Lucas."

Pink rose to the surface of Ruby's cheeks and her shoulders drew tight. "But it's not exactly the same, is it? I was going to spend the rest of my life with Lucas. My entire future was wrapped up in him. He took a piece of my heart with him. It will never be replaced. There will always be a part of me that is missing. And it's not coming back."

"Are you trying to say that romantic love is stronger than what I had for my family? I don't see how that makes any sense. Family is the beginning and the end."

"Family is about more than blood, Heath. It's about love and trust. You can make someone your family. You can also send them away."

"Well, that much is true. My brother did that."

"Please don't feel sorry for yourself."

"I'm not. These are facts." The frustration inside was so immense that he could hardly think straight. "You know, Ruby, you told me that you were disappointed in me, but I have to say that I feel the same way about you. You have always understood my side in this. What changed? What's different?"

She scanned his face as if she were looking for answers or deciphering a puzzle. "It's different because I love you."

Heath blinked several times. *That* he had not expected. And he didn't know how to respond. He was incredibly fond of Ruby. His mind and body wanted her. Needed her. But love? Already? It hadn't even been a month. He wasn't ready to say that, especially when she was so angry with him.

Ruby laughed quietly, but nothing about the situation was funny. "Okay, then. This is just like me. To go and fall in love with a man who I thought I knew, only to find out that he's a stranger. It's like I lost you, Heath. Just like I lost Lucas."

"And I'd like a minute to catch up, if that's okay with you." He kneaded his forehead. "Plus, isn't that a little melodramatic? We're having an argument. I'm not going anywhere."

"But I am." She leaned closer and kissed him on the cheek. "Take care of yourself. Please. Promise me that much." She opened her door.

"What are you saying?"

She hopped out of the truck and turned back to him, holding the door and boring into his soul with those brilliant green eyes of hers. "I can't do this, Heath. I can't. I need someone who's looking ahead to the future, not focused on the past. The past is where all of my hurt is. I need to keep that where it is. Behind me." She closed the door and headed for her car.

Heath wasn't ready for this to be over. He couldn't let her leave. He leaped out of the truck and ran over to her. "You tell me you love me one minute, and in the next, you tell me it's over?"

She opened her car door and climbed inside, immediately turning on the engine. "And you didn't say a damn thing back to me. That told me all I needed to know."

"I need time, Ruby. That's all. I care about you a lot." *So much. More than anyone. Including myself.*

"Now you'll have all the time you need." With that, she closed her car door and sped down his driveway, kicking up gravel.

As Ruby disappeared in a cloud of dust, traveling away from his house and from him, it felt like she was dragging his heart behind her car. Part of him was gone now. It might never come back. It sent his mind into a downward spiral of pure chaos. And the one sentiment it kept circling back to was that the only reason he felt like this was that he loved her. He. Loved. Her. *Dammit. Dammit. Dammit. Why in the hell is my heart on a ten-minute delay?* He wanted to kick himself. If he could have figured out a way to make his boot meet his ass, he would have done it. More than once. He probably wouldn't have felt it, though. His body was too numb. He'd thought he'd experienced loss before, but this was something entirely different. It was like the earth had been yanked out from under his feet and now he was floating in space, aimless, with nothing or no one to rescue him. He'd been on his own before and he did not want to go back to being that man again. Moving forward? He couldn't do that if he didn't have Ruby.

He bent over and rested his hands on his knees, letting the cold work its way through his clothes and wondering what came next. Go inside? What was the point? His whole life had fallen apart, and either he was going to salvage it and piece it back together, or he was going to accept defeat. People had said countless horrible things about him, but one thing no one could dispute was that he was determined.

He climbed back in his truck and wasted no time getting to the main road. When he came to the stop, he had enough presence of mind to carefully look both ways. If he turned left, he'd be headed to Ruby's. But what could they possibly argue about now? He had to move the needle. He had to prove to her that he was the man she'd fallen in love with, not the man who mindlessly sought vengeance. Which meant he needed to turn right. That direction would eventually lead him to a place he did not want to go. A place he'd once been convinced was where pure evil resided. The instant the idea came into his head, he wanted to bat it away like a fly. But there was no other way. If he wanted to fix his relationship with his brother and convince Ruby that he really was the man she needed him to be, he was going to have to go through hell to do it.

With resignation so deep it registered as a burning ache in his belly, he sucked in a sharp breath, flipped on his turn signal and headed in the direction away from Ruby. He went right. Straight toward the Grandin family ranch.

Eleven

Heath's meeting with the Grandins never happened. They wouldn't even let him through the gates. Instead, Vic rode out on a horse and told Heath to get off their property. The *hell* off their *damn* property, to be exact.

So Heath shifted to plan B, which was to convince Albert to meet him on his day off, so they could discuss their options for getting Nelson Redfield to back off. They arranged a call with the man, and that was when Heath met his second roadblock—the county attorney was not playing around. He'd seen the original survey and he'd seen a copy of the oil rights, and although he refused to divulge his source, he wanted Heath to know that he agreed with him. The Grandins and the Lattimores had purposely deceived his mother, and his sister had been denied her birthright.

"You should be happy," he'd said to Heath. "They're finally going to pay for what they did."

To which Heath replied, "Except that I'm not. I don't want the Grandins or the Lattimores to get into trouble over this. What's done is done. It's water under the bridge." He could hardly believe those words had come out of his mouth, but it was his determination, and stubbornness, talking. He would do anything to fix this, all so he had a chance of fixing his relationship with Nolan and getting Ruby back.

"It's an election year, Mr. Thurston," Nelson said. "I can't drop it now. My constituents need to know I'm tough on crime. Any chance you'd be interested in a donation? We can always stand to print more yard signs when the time comes."

"I'm going to forget that you asked my client for money," Albert said right before he ended the call. Then he turned to Heath. "He wants a high-profile case to campaign on. That's all this is. Nelson Redfield cares about justice about as much as I care about losing weight and exercising more."

That gave Heath an idea. "Who's his opponent?"

"You want to dabble in local politics? That's a dangerous game."

Heath shrugged it off. Nothing could make his predicament worse. "I've been playing with fire this whole time."

That had been a week ago, which meant it had been that long since Heath had seen Ruby. Every day had been a test of his mental toughness. It was so hard not to see her, especially knowing that she was so nearby. He'd left a few messages for her, all of which hadn't been returned. He missed her so desperately that it felt like his entire body was hollow. He was a shell of a man, fueled by nothing other than tenacity and a refusal to fail. He would not let the actions of the old Heath steal the future the new Heath wanted, which was to be with Ruby. Forever.

As for that part, although he had left her those messages, he hadn't divulged the full breadth of his feelings. It didn't feel right to say it over the phone. He wanted to say it to her beautiful face. He needed to witness her reaction, if only to know that all of this had been worthwhile. He did manage to gather one piece of intel as to what she was up to—he'd gone to the hardware store to get a new latch for Lucky's stall door, and the woman working the register, who apparently had seen Ruby and Heath together at the Royal Diner, told him that he'd just missed her. She'd been in for some paint and drywall mud. It was nice to know what she was doing, but it also made him incredibly sad. She worked on her house when she was feeling down and lost. He hated the thought of her being unhappy. He knew that he could make things better for her, but the key to that was repairing the damage he'd done.

The real work of that was going to happen today, more than a week after the awful news of the criminal case had broken. He was about to do one more thing he'd never *ever* thought he would do. He was about to welcome the Grandins and the Lattimores to his home. This was not going to be a social visit, but he still felt as though he had to offer refreshments, so he was putting out tea and a cheese board with crackers. Also a bottle of bourbon because he was certainly going to need it. The hospitality was all his mother's doing. She might have struggled her whole life, but she was a Southern woman through and through, and she always offered guests a beverage and a snack of some sort. Always.

Heath hoped to hell this was going to work. No, he hadn't been successful in reaching Ruby and inviting her to come to this event, but he had at least convinced his brother and Chelsea. Although, to be fair, Nolan hadn't needed much persuading. He was desperate for all of this to go away. During the most recent phone conversation they'd had, Nolan had even expressed to Heath that he believed him. Nolan said he'd been angry when they were at the Rancher's Daughter, but it had subsided, which gave Heath something to cling to. Someone was on his side, and that person was immensely important to him—his twin brother.

Chelsea and Nolan were the first to arrive. Nolan offered a handshake rather than a hug, but Heath knew it was going to take time for their brotherly relationship to get fully back on the right track.

"I hope this works," Chelsea said, casting Heath a doubtful look.

"Alexa seemed happy with everything when she and I talked," Heath said. Alexa was a Lattimore, the elder daughter, who was a lawyer and representing the Grandin and Lattimore families.

"I'm glad to hear that. Alexa's a hard nut to crack. If she's happy, that gives me some optimism," Chelsea said, glancing at Nolan. "By the way, do you have a place where we can set up a laptop? My uncle Daniel wants to join us via videoconference."

Now, this was a new development. Daniel was the man believed to be Ashley's father, who lived in France and had very little interaction with the rest of the Grandin family. "Is there something I need to know?" Heath asked.

"Only that he wants to be involved. And I believe he has something he wants to say to you and Nolan." Chelsea reached for Heath's arm. It was a small gesture, but it meant the world to him. "Don't worry. I think it'll all be good. Barbara Lattimore reached out to him after she talked to Alexa. She likes bringing people together."

"Okay. Sounds good. We can set up the laptop on the entertainment center in the living room."

"I'll take care of that," Nolan said. "Have you talked to Ruby?"

Heath shook his head. "I haven't. I called and left a few messages, but she hasn't returned my call. I'm just hoping she doesn't hate me. Although, I would understand it if she did. I messed up. I made a huge mistake and I was wrong. That's what today is for. Apologies. I have a lot of them to make." He glanced out the window and his heart immediately started pounding. Out in his driveway was Victor Grandin Jr., Vic and Chelsea's father, and his wife, Bethany. Heath looked at Chelsea and Nolan. "I guess this is starting. Wish me luck."

Without hesitating, he headed for his front door, opened it and stepped out onto the porch. Ben and Barbara Lattimore, along with their daughter Alexa, were climbing out of their car. It was a surreal moment for Heath, standing there and facing the people who he'd been at war with, knowing that he was about to extend the olive branch and try like hell to make this all go away. "Thank you for coming. Please, come inside and grab a drink, and we'll get started."

Barbara Lattimore led the way, marching right up to Heath with her husband, Ben, right behind her. "Mr. Thurston," Barbara said. "My husband and I look forward to hearing what you have to say."

Heath shook hands with them both. "Call me Heath. I hope that we can all part ways today with a clear path forward."

Their daughter Alexa joined them and shook hands

with Heath. "It's nice to see you, Heath. Are we all good with the plan we discussed?"

Heath nodded eagerly. "Absolutely. Nolan and Chelsea have already arrived." The three strolled past him, leaving Heath to greet Victor Jr. and Bethany. "Mr. and Mrs. Grandin. Thank you for coming."

Victor Jr. glanced at his wife, then turned his attention to Heath, offering a firm handshake. "It takes a big man to do what you're doing."

Heath finally felt as though he could breathe. This wasn't going to be easy, but it was already going far better than he ever could've imagined. He let the last of his guests walk inside. Then he followed and closed the door. Everyone was either helping themselves to refreshments or had already settled in the living room, which was where Heath had planned to talk.

"Game time?" Nolan said, handing his brother a small glass of bourbon.

"I believe so."

"Good. I got Daniel all set up on the laptop. He's on right now. Good luck."

Heath slugged back his drink for courage, then strolled into the room and stood near the fireplace, which gave Daniel Grandin a good view of all in attendance. "I'm going to make this quick and to the point. I'd like to say that I made a mistake, but that's not entirely accurate. I've made dozens." He paused, soaking up the admission. "I led a vengeful crusade against your two families and it was wrong. I allowed my actions to be determined by anger and I didn't listen when anyone tried to point out the harm I was inflicting. And so I'd like to apologize. I am sorry for any and all pain I have caused. I am truly sorry." Heath took a moment to let the relief of getting that off his chest roll over him. A weight had been lifted. Already.

"Thank you, Heath. I think both families appreciate that," Alexa said.

"Well, I hope so. And if anyone needs to speak to me privately after this, please don't hesitate to ask." He drew in one more deep breath. "Which brings me to my plans to get Nelson Redfield to back off." With that announcement, everyone seemed to lean in to listen more closely. Heath went on to explain the complications of it being an election year and that he believed the county attorney's motivations were purely political. "Running for this office is all about holding on to power. Nelson Redfield has held this position for over twenty years, and I think everyone in this room knows that he really only surfaces when it's time to be reelected. No one has made a serious run at unseating him, but there's an amazing candidate named Lucia Vega up against him. Alexa speaks very highly of her. She's smart and young and she's hungry to go after real crime in our county. I'd like to encourage everyone in this room to throw their support behind Ms. Vega. It will be one part of the two-pronged approach I devised to get Mr. Redfield to drop his case."

"What's the other half of it?" Barbara asked.

"The other half is a PR campaign. Your two families are beloved in this community," Heath said. "Believe me. The ire I received by going after you was fierce. So let's let Nelson Redfield know that his plan is not going to be a popular one. We do that by publicly reminding everyone of your importance to Royal. Which is why I'd like to invite you to partner with my brother and me in the development of the Ashley Thurston Therapeutic Riding Center." Heath explained the mission of the center, as well as its financial needs. "I think it's a win-win for everyone. And of course, any donation will be fully tax-deductible."

Barbara looked at her husband and they both smiled. Then Ben turned to Heath. "We're in. You can count on the full support of the Lattimore family."

Victor Jr., who had been silent up until this point, cleared his throat. "We are, too. Of course." He directed his attention to Nolan and Chelsea. "I mostly just want Chelsea and our new son-in-law to know that we care and want to be a part of making things better between the families."

Heath breathed a huge sigh of relief. "This is fantastic. And I think it's the right call. My mother and sister might be gone, but this is the right thing to do in their memory." It was an immensely difficult thing to say. For as many times as he'd said that he was moving on from the deaths of his mother and sister, he hadn't really. That was the crux of why he'd been pursuing all of this. It had been too hard to accept that they were gone. "We have to move forward. This will pave the way."

"I believe my uncle Daniel would like to say something," Chelsea said.

Daniel straightened in his seat and leaned closer to his computer monitor. "Hey, y'all. I won't take up too much of your time. Heath and Nolan, I just want you to know that I truly did not know about Ashley. I had no idea, and I'm very sorry that I never got to know her. By all accounts, she was a lovely human being."

Yet again, Heath was confronted with the other side of the story. Ashley had missed out, but so had Daniel. He'd had a daughter who he hadn't had the privilege of knowing.

"What your mother and I shared was very nice, but it was fleeting," Daniel continued. "I was young and so was she. I honestly thought it was nothing more than a fling, and so I moved on. If I had known that she'd had a child and that she was mine, I would have come back to Royal. I would have proudly taken responsibility. And so I'm happy to contribute whatever you need to make Ashley's riding center a reality. And someday, I'd like to learn more about her from you both, Heath and Nolan. In the meantime, just tell me what you need and I'll make sure you get it."

Heath looked at Nolan and an entire conversation took place in a split second, all without words. Emotion welled up in Heath's eyes, but he kept it at bay.

"I have something that needs to be said as well." Barbara stood and looked at everyone in the room, one by one. She was an admirable woman, someone who did not beat around the bush or mince words. "My husband and I have talked about this a great deal. And I spoke to Miriam about it as well." Miriam Grandin was the matriarch of that family, in her late eighties. She was the widow of Victor Grandin Sr., who had died nine months ago, right before the question of the oil rights had come up. "Victor Sr. and Augustus Lattimore, my father-in-law, may have led the families well for decades, but they were misguided in many of their actions. What they did to cover up the birth of Ashley and her true family lineage was disgraceful. And every last person in this room has had to suffer because of it in one way or another. We can't go back and undo the past, but if we acknowledge it, we can heal. I think Heath has laid out a road map for us to follow, and I think we all need to thank him for that."

Heath was so choked up he could hardly see straight. The last thing he'd ever imagined was that anyone would thank him for anything. "I don't need the praise, but I do appreciate it. Really."

Barbara looked around the room one more time. "Can we toast to it? Because I think we could all use a drink."

Ruby was trying to finish up the last of the painting in her new closet, but she kept making mistakes. "Dammit," she muttered as she once again slipped with the roller and left a big smudge on the ceiling. "I'm going to have so much touch-up to do. It's ridiculous." Of course, it wasn't entirely a case of being clumsy. She was on edge. Chelsea had called her that morning to let Ruby know that Heath was having the Grandins and the Lattimores over to the Thurston ranch today so they could discuss a plan to get the county attorney to drop the case against the families.

Ruby could only imagine what might be going on. Screaming. Yelling. Throwing of sharp objects. Funnily enough, as much as Heath had been blamed for all of this, she didn't see him doing those things. No, she imagined him sitting at one end of one of the couches in his living room, patiently listening and waiting until there was a break in the conversation so that he could tell everyone why they were wrong. He was very good at arguing. So much so that Ruby had thought he might have a future as a lawyer.

She felt bad about everything that had happened. She knew that she'd been particularly hard on him when they'd had their argument in his driveway after the dustup at the Rancher's Daughter. Even so, nothing she'd said was untrue. She did need to move forward, and everything in Heath's actions had said that he wasn't ready to do that. But she still wondered if maybe this had been a stumbling block for him. That although there was a difference between what he did and what he said, it didn't change what he wanted. There was a very good chance that his desire to move ahead was real, but he hadn't known the right way to go about it.

The many messages he'd left for her had hinted at all of that. As reluctant as she'd been to take his calls, she did listen to the things he had to say. More than once. Sometimes she listened to them right before she went to bed, if only to have the comfort of his voice in the dark. He did sound sad. And he did sound sincere. But something was keeping her from reaching out to him. And she wasn't sure what it was.

She finished up the last of the painting, then gathered her supplies and went into her laundry room to wash things up in the utility tub. With that done, she went next to the living room to look at the clothes she'd piled on the sofa. Some of these things probably needed to be donated to the thrift store in town. As she sifted through the garments, she came across the dress that Heath had bought for her to wear to the party at the TCC. And it really struck her exactly how generous it had been of him to buy it for her. What was between them was so new at that point, and although there had been physical intimacy, she had stomped on the brakes, which he'd taken in stride. He had an immense capacity to understand and to be giving, even when the world had not always shown him those positive traits. When she'd told him that he was a good man, she'd been right. And she'd meant it.

The sound of Ruby's cell phone ringing took her by surprise. She flipped through the pile of clothes until she found the device. The caller ID said it was Chelsea. "Hey. Is everything okay? Did anyone end up in the hospital?" Ruby didn't want to sound melodramatic, but considering the outlandish things that had happened in the last month, it wasn't completely out of the question.

"No. Actually, everything is great. I can hardly believe I'm saying that, but it's true. Heath and Nolan are in the other room with my dad and mom, and Barbara and Ben Lattimore. They're chatting up a storm and having a great time."

Ruby struggled to understand how such a dramatic shift could have taken place. "What happened?"

"It's a long story, but the short version is that Heath worked his butt off to come up with a way out of this. And he apologized to everyone in a very beautiful way. He was so humble, and, well, he just basically proved to us all what an incredible man he is."

Ruby was so thrilled to hear this news, but it came

at a price. "I feel horrible. He's been trying to reach me all week and I haven't called him back."

"He told us. You didn't want to talk to him?"

"It's not that. Actually, I think I just needed time to process my feelings. I'm a work in progress. There's not much more I can say than that."

"We all are, aren't we?"

"True. Very true." Ruby smiled, but it faded quickly. "And there's one other thing. I told him that I love him and he didn't say it back. It's hard to recover from that."

Chelsea's end of the line was quiet for a moment. "Can I tell you something about the Thurston men? They aren't great at admitting to their feelings. At least, not right away. I have zero doubt that he cares about you a lot. And that he wants to see you. I really think his actions today were motivated so much by his feelings for you. So, maybe give him another chance?"

Ruby really wanted to, but would it work? She wasn't sure. "I should at least talk to him, right?"

"Yes. Get your butt over here and talk to him. I know he would love to see you and it would absolutely make his day. It'll probably make his whole life."

"I just finished a painting job. I need to get cleaned up. It'll probably be an hour or so."

"From the sound of the laughter coming from the other room, I don't think he's going anywhere. Just get here when you can."

Ruby smiled, happy to have a way forward. "I

will. And thank you, Chelsea. I really appreciate you reaching out."

"I like you a lot, Ruby. I hope you and Heath can sort it out. Then we can hopefully go shopping at the Rancher's Daughter and not have anything horrible happen."

"That sounds like fun." Ruby said goodbye to Chelsea, hung up the phone and headed straight for her bathroom. She showered as quickly as she could, nervous anticipation running through her body at full speed. She hoped that Heath would talk to her. She hoped that he would give her a chance to apologize, and hopefully that would mean a second chance at them being a couple. She dressed in jeans and the same sweater she'd been wearing the day they met. It was a sentimental choice, harking back to the beginning. As much as she'd told him it was important to move forward, it was okay to look back sometimes. Hair and makeup took a bit longer than she would have liked, but she wanted to look good. A final spritz of perfume and she was ready to go.

She stopped at the front door to pull on her boots, but something caught her eye as she glimpsed the living room—the bar cabinet. Lucas's bourbon collection was in there. Heath was its rightful owner, as far as she was concerned. Lucas would have wanted a true connoisseur to have it. She ran back to the guest room, grabbed an empty cardboard box and started carefully packing up the bottles. With that complete, she felt as though she could leave.

With a click of her fob, she raised the tailgate on her SUV and was sliding the box into the back when she heard a car kicking up gravel on her road. She turned and saw Heath's big black truck coming toward her. She was more than a little confounded. Chelsea had said he was busy socializing at the house. When had he decided to leave? And why had he decided to come here?

He parked right alongside her car and hopped out. "Please don't tell me you're moving, Ruby. Why are you loading boxes into your car?"

A grin crossed her face, and she sighed for good measure. He was so handsome it was worth marking the moment. "Not moving. I was bringing you a gift."

He stepped closer and glanced in the back of her car, then looked at her with pure astonishment on his face. "The bourbon collection? For me?"

She grasped his arm, needing to touch him. "I figured I had to apologize. I shouldn't have gotten so upset with you that day. I should have given you the benefit of the doubt. I'm so sorry."

Heath shook his head so fast it messed up his hair. "No. Ruby. I'm the one who's sorry. And before we get any deeper into this conversation, can I please just tell you that I love you?"

The words went into her ears, registered in her brain, and the next thing she knew, she was flattening herself against his solid chest and wrapping her arms around his waist. "You do?"

He pulled her in even tighter, kissing the top of her head. "I knew that I loved you, but I hadn't admitted it to myself. I think I never thought that you would fall for me. I always thought I would be the one doing the falling."

Ruby reared back her head. "What? Did you really think that?"

He nodded. "I did. I'm not always the sharpest tool in the shed."

A laugh escaped her lips. "Oh, shush. You're brilliant. From everything Chelsea said, you really saved the day today. I can't believe you figured it all out."

"Chelsea called you?"

"She did. I think she feels just as bad about everything that happened that day at Morgan's shop."

"Maybe we should forget the whole thing."

"I think that sounds like an excellent idea."

"Well, we're not out of the woods yet, but I think we have a solid plan, and most important, we're all on the same page. No more warring between families."

She smiled and peered up into his face. It was a chilly afternoon, but she didn't care. Heath was all of the warmth she needed. "That's so great. I don't want there to be any more war. All I want is peace and happiness. Especially between us."

"Good. Because that's exactly what I want, too."

He brushed aside a lock of her hair. "You and I have talked so many times about how hard it is to say goodbye. But I don't ever want to say goodbye to you, Ruby." Pulling her closer, he planted a soft and sensuous kiss on her lips. "Tell me I don't have to say goodbye."

Ruby was nearly floating from the kiss. "From now on, we only say hello."

Epilogue

Seven months later

Heath had hoped for better weather today, but apparently that wasn't meant to be.

"Clouds? How can it be this overcast in the middle of August in Texas?" he asked Ruby as he poured himself a cup of coffee and peered out through the kitchen window. This view out onto his property was especially beautiful this time of year, with the meadow of perennial wildflowers planted by his mother years ago in full bloom. August was one of his favorite months in Royal. He loved the first taste of summer heat, the way the air was sweet and sticky, but not quite suffocating yet. "It's supposed to be a happy day. When I think of happy, I think of sunshine."

"It *will* be a happy day, regardless of whether or not there are a few clouds." Ruby was seated at the kitchen island, drinking coffee and reading on her phone.

Of course, she was right. And in many ways, she was the only sunshine he needed. "Thank you for telling me to stop being so negative without actually pointing out that I was in fact being negative."

"That's my job. Kindly putting you on notice." She cleared her throat and slid her mug across the kitchen island. "Like now. Refill, please."

He happily obliged her request, then walked the cup around to her. "What if it rains?"

"Then it rains and people get wet if they don't bring an umbrella."

"Should we call everyone and tell them to bring one?"

Ruby sighed and set her phone aside. "I know you want everything to be perfect, but it's not possible, okay? It doesn't mean today won't be great. I promise it will." She ended her long string of assertions with a smile, probably knowing he could never disagree with her when she had that look on her face.

Indeed, he did want the opening of the Ashley Thurston Therapeutic Riding Center to be perfect. But simply the fact that they'd gotten this far was enough. "I'm so glad you're here for this. I couldn't do it without you." He couldn't fathom what today would be like without her. "Now we should probably sit down and look through the to-do list. Just to make sure we don't miss anything."

Ruby dropped her head to one side. "Heath. Do you really think I would let anything go undone? I want you to enjoy today. This is your victory lap. Take it. I promise you that everything will be perfect."

Good God, he loved her so much. She was the one person on the planet who enjoyed taking care of him. It was such a delicious change of pace. He'd spent his first thirty-three years on this earth worrying about others. "Have I told you lately how much I love you?"

She smiled. "Last night before we went to bed, but I wouldn't mind hearing it again."

"I love you, Ruby Rose Bennett. More than you will ever know." Although, Heath had a plan for later today that involved showing her exactly how much he loved her. And he hoped like hell that it would be met with an affirmative response. He didn't know what he would do if she said no.

"I love you, too, Heath. I hope you know that."

"I do, but just like you, I also enjoy hearing it on a regular basis."

An alarm on his smartwatch went off. "Can you at least run me through the schedule for today?"

"Of course." Ruby sipped her coffee. "The caterer arrives at ten. They'll be setting up everything. Lunch, the bar, the tables and chairs out on the back patio. Guests arrive at eleven. The signs are all posted to direct everyone to park at the riding center. You'll give your speech. We'll do the ribbon cutting. Then you and Nolan can give everyone a quick tour of the stables and the riding corrals, and everyone will get to meet the horses, too."

"I still can't believe I have to make a speech."

"After everything everyone has been through, I think it's only fitting that you're the one to finally put the last positive spin on everything."

Heath sucked in a deep breath, fighting back the nerves that threatened his morning calm. "I suppose you're right."

"Then after that, everyone will drive back up here to the house. The caterer will have everything ready, so all we need to do is have lunch and socialize. I think we should be all done by two or three at the latest, depending on how long everyone decides to stay."

As thrilled as Heath was about everything today, he was nervous about the socializing part. It had been about two months since the county attorney had officially dropped the case against the Grandin and Lattimore families, but he still worried about whether enough time had passed for everyone to feel as though they could truly move on. "I can't wait until this is over."

"But you've been looking forward to it for weeks."

"I know. But I also just want to move ahead and get to the business of doing the actual work. You know, getting the people who will benefit from this here onto the ranch and riding. That's all that matters to me."

"And that's why I love you, Heath Thurston. You don't care about the spotlight. You care about getting things done."

"Exactly why I'm not super excited to give a speech."

"Which is why I'm here. To force you to do things you don't want to do. Like go get in the shower. Your brother and Chelsea are going to be here in forty-five minutes."

"You don't want to join me?" he asked with a bob of his eyebrows.

"Normally, yes. But I have things I need to do."

It was probably for the best. If he was going to have that time with her, he didn't want to rush. "I'll go get ready."

"Sounds good."

Heath walked down to their bedroom and got cleaned up, then dressed in a pale blue dress shirt and dark jeans, trying to strike the balance between looking nice, staying cool, and recognizing that he was going to have to show folks around a horse barn in a few hours. By the time he walked back out to the main part of the house, he saw that the caterers had arrived early and had already taken over his kitchen. Outside, they were setting up a tent to provide respite from the August sun, and luckily enough, protection from the rain if they needed it.

"This is a bit of a surprise," he said to Ruby.

"Tell me about it. I guess better early than late, but I still need to get dressed."

"You go. I'll be here if anyone has any questions."

Ruby popped up onto her tiptoes and kissed his cheek. "I'll be right back."

Heath walked out to the back patio. The caterers were setting up tables and bringing in all sorts of supplies for lunch. He kept waiting for someone to ask him a question, but Ruby had apparently done an excellent job in preparing them. They knew exactly what they were doing, so he walked back inside. He stopped at the built-in cabinets in the living room, opened a drawer and peeked inside, just to make sure a very important item was still there. He was about to pull it out when he heard Nolan's voice.

"Knock, knock," Nolan said.

Heath slammed the drawer closed and hustled into the foyer, watching as Nolan closed the door behind Chelsea.

"Hey, you two," Heath said, embracing his brother and then Chelsea. "Ruby should be out in a second."

"I'm right here," Ruby said, emerging from the hall that went back to the master bedroom. She gave Nolan and Chelsea a hug, then stepped to Heath's side.

"So, we have news. And we thought now was a

good time to deliver it," Nolan said, looking conspiratorially at Chelsea.

"I'm pregnant!" Chelsea exclaimed.

Heath didn't know who to hug first, but since Ruby immediately descended on Chelsea, that left his brother. As they embraced, Heath was overwhelmed with gratitude and joy, while he was also struck by the feeling that their mom and sister should be here for this. It brought a bittersweet edge to an otherwise perfect moment. "I am *so* happy for you guys," Heath said.

Chelsea smiled and touched her belly. "It's still early. I'm about three months along."

"A winter baby. How exciting," Ruby said.

"We're really happy. Now we just need to get our house going. As you know, we haven't had any luck pinning down our contractor on a start date, and the lease on the loft is just about up. We need to figure out a plan," Nolan said.

"We do *not* want to move in with my parents. I love them, but no," Chelsea added. "And of course, my real worry is that we won't have a place to be settled in when the baby comes."

That gave Heath an idea, but he was going to need to speak to Ruby about it first. "Well, congratulations. It's really amazing."

"We should probably head down to the stables," Ruby said. "We don't want the guests arriving before us."

"Good point," Heath said.

The four of them piled into Heath's truck and rode down one of the access roads that bisected the ranch until they were at the far end of the property. Heath wasn't sure he'd ever tire of seeing the riding center now that it was complete. There was the welcome center, complete with classrooms, offices for staff and other administrative purposes. The stable was state-of-the-art with full climate control for the horses and easy access for loading in feed. Beyond that were three corrals—one open-air, one covered and another that was fully enclosed so that the center could be used year-round. Heath had spared no expense in making his sister's dream come to life. He hoped it would be standing for a very long time.

Ruby was so full of pride for Heath's accomplishment when they arrived at the riding center that she felt like her heart might burst. It was such an honor to be part of this momentous day.

"It's so beautiful," Chelsea said when they got out of the truck.

"My brother did a fantastic job," Nolan said, clapping Heath on the back.

"We *both* did a fantastic job. It was a joint effort. As it should have been."

Off in the distance, Ruby saw a car turn onto the main access road for the riding center. "It looks like the first of the guests are here."

"That's Ryan and Morgan in that first car. I can't wait to love on my niece," Chelsea said as Nolan and Heath walked toward the main corral.

Ruby hadn't even known that Morgan was pregnant when she first met her, but she was. Morgan had given birth to a little girl named Cora about two weeks ago. Ruby had only seen her a few times, but she had the most adorable head of bright red hair, just like her mama. "There's Alexa and Jackson," Ruby said, referring to Alexa Lattimore and her husband, Jackson Strom. "Hold on a minute. Is that a baby bump I see?"

Chelsea elbowed Ruby. "Yes. Morgan told me Alexa is pregnant. It's a bit surprising. She doesn't seem like the mommy type, but apparently they're very happy."

"That's so great," Ruby said. "Looks like we're about to have a real crowd." She pointed at the growing line of cars pulling up the drive to the parking lot. "I'd better go talk to Heath about his speech."

Ruby found Heath and Nolan down in the spot where they planned to do the dedication, in a lovely grassy spot. Right next to it was the main corral, which was occupied solely by Lucky. Heath thought she should be there to represent Ashley. The brothers were both stroking Lucky's head.

"Everyone will be here any minute."

Heath looked past her. "Looks to me like we've already got a capacity crowd. It's Grandins and Lattimores for days. Even Daniel Grandin flew in from Paris."

That alone was full evidence of just how much things had changed in the last seven months. When she'd met Heath, those names were like poison in his mouth. Now he talked about them like friends, and there was zero controversy in bringing up the topic. It was such a welcome relief. "Are you nervous?"

Heath was wringing his hands. "A little. Like I said earlier, I want to get past this part. So we can get on with our life." He pulled Ruby closer and kissed her cheek. "Thank you for being here today. I couldn't do any of this without you."

"It's my absolute pleasure. And just so you know, I think your speech is going to be fantastic." Ruby strode over to the arriving guests, waving them closer and directing them where to stand. Heath had been adamant about no chairs, since he wanted this to be very short and sweet. After ten minutes or so, it seemed as though everyone was ready. Ruby gave Heath the go-ahead with a nod of her head.

"Thank you, everyone, for coming today as we mark the opening of the Ashley Thurston Therapeutic Riding Center. My brother, Nolan, and I are so happy that you could join us for this important day. As many of you know, this was a dream of our sister's, and it means a lot to be able to bring it to fruition, for the enjoyment of the entire Royal community. It would not have been possible without the generous donations of both the Grandin and Lattimore families. I want to give special thanks to Vic Grandin, who called in many favors with his friends in construction. Vic made our impossibly tight deadline possible." Everyone in the crowd clapped, no one as much as Heath did. He and Vic had actually become friends, which was its own miracle. "So I hope everyone will enjoy a quick tour of the facilities and then join us up at the house for lunch."

Another round of applause followed the end of Heath's speech, and then everyone descended upon him and Nolan. Ruby hung back, letting Heath have his moment in the sun, and just enjoying watching him as he gave tours and talked about bringing Ashley's vision to life. It was so endearing to see the time and attention he gave to everyone he interacted with. One thing no one could accuse Heath Thurston of was being ungenerous.

After an hour or so, everyone drove up to the house, where they all had a lovely lunch of what Ruby had learned was Ashley's favorite midday meal, a chicken Caesar salad with warm yeast rolls and iced tea, followed by his mother's favorite dessert, lemon icebox pie. It all went off without a hitch, exactly as Ruby had planned it. Bellies full and hearts bursting with the loveliness of the day, one by one the guests all said goodbye. Nolan and Chelsea were the last to leave.

"Goodbye, Nolan," Heath said. "We did good today."

"You did good, brother. And I couldn't be any more proud."

Ruby and Chelsea watched as they shared an extended embrace. It was a touching moment, in the midst of a day chock-full of happy times. "I hope you continue to feel well," Ruby said to Chelsea.

"Thanks. I'd love your help picking out baby clothes, if you're ever up for more shopping."

Ruby hugged Chelsea. "Sounds great. Text me."

Heath and Ruby stood in the driveway and watched as his brother and Chelsea drove away. Then they headed back inside. Now that everyone had gone, Ruby wanted a chance to bring something up with Heath, but she was a little nervous about it. He'd been so stressed about today. Unveiling the riding center had been a massive undertaking, right on the heels of building it. Maybe it wasn't best to put a big question in his lap. Would he think it was too soon? Would he think she was moving too fast? "Hey, Heath. I was thinking about something," she said as they walked into the kitchen.

"Oh, no. Not that." He reined her in with his strong arms, the one place she always wanted to be.

"Stop joking around. I'm serious."

He adopted a far more stern look on his face. His forehead wrinkled with concern. "Okay. Go."

"Well, I can't stop thinking about what Nolan and Chelsea said. That the contractor can't start on their house yet. With the baby coming, I know that's got to be incredibly stressful for Chelsea. And let's face it, even if they broke ground today, there's no way a custom home is going to be ready to move into in six months. You had to move heaven and earth to get the riding center built in that time, and that didn't require everything a home will."

"Right. And it's pretty clear that she hates the idea of having to move back home with her parents." Heath pressed his lips together tightly. "I was thinking about suggesting that they come and live here, but I wanted to talk to you about it first. I wouldn't want to make a decision like that without you."

"Well, I actually had a different idea. What if we let Nolan and Chelsea move into my house? It's completely finished and the perfect size for a young family. They could set up a real nursery and have their own space."

A deep crease formed between Heath's eyes. "So you're saying you want to move in here?"

Ruby was confounded by his tone. It was so stern. "I am. But hold on. What did you mean when you said that you wouldn't want to invite them to live here without talking to me first? It's your house."

Heath pinched the bridge of his nose. "I should know better than to plan anything. It never works out exactly the way I want it to." He started for the living room. "Come on."

"Heath. What is going on?" she asked, shuffling after him. "Are you angry? Are you upset with me?"

He stopped in front of the entertainment center,

but didn't turn back to her. "No. Quite the contrary. But I need you to stop talking and close your eyes."

"Now I'm super confused."

"Like I said, no talking."

"Okay. My lips are sealed." Ruby stood as still as a statue, unsure what he was doing, but trusting that there was a reason behind his strange behavior.

"Okay," Heath said. His voice was inches away. "Open your eyes."

Ruby gasped. There before her was Heath on bended knee with a small box from a jewelry store in his hand. "Heath. Is this why you've been acting so antsy today?"

"Yes. The stuff with the riding center was fine. This was the real thing I was nervous about." He smiled and encouraged her with a nod of his head. "Please. Open it."

She took the box from his hands and popped it open. Inside was a beautiful solitaire diamond, surrounded by rubies, in a platinum setting. It was so beautiful, she couldn't even touch it. Nor did she know what to say.

"I don't just want you to think about moving in, Ruby. I want to know if you'll marry me."

She blinked at him as tears started to roll down her cheeks. "I...I..." No matter how hard she tried, the words would not come out.

"Hold on. I just want to say one more thing."

"Before you do that, will you please stand up?"

"I thought you'd never ask. These floors are murder on my knee." He straightened to his full height and gathered himself, then took her hand. "Today was a chance for me to honor two very important women in my life. But I'm hoping that you'll become the most important woman in my world. My wife. Will you marry me?"

She nodded so many times she was surprised she wasn't flinging tears all over the room. With one hand, she took the box with the ring in it, and with the other, she clasped the side of his head and brought his lips to hers. "I love you so much, Heath. Of course I will marry you. I can't wait to marry you."

He took the ring from the box and slid it onto her hand. She wiggled her fingers, watching the beautiful stones catch the light. "I not only went with rubies because of your name, but you also told me you were a nerd for rocks. These are the best rocks I could find."

She giggled so hard she nearly couldn't stop. "You can be a real goof, Heath. And I love you for it."

He laughed quietly. "I'll take goof over bullheaded any day. And I love you, too, Ruby Rose Bennett. More than you'll ever know."

* * * * *

Return to Royal, Texas, with
Texas Cattleman's Club: The Wedding

Reese Ryan launches the new series with
A Cowboy Kind of Thing

Available February 2023!

#2923 ONE NIGHT RANCHER

The Carsons of Lone Rock • by Maisey Yates

To buy the property, bar owner Cara Thompson must spend one night at a ghostly hotel and asks her best friend, Jace Carson, to join her. But when forbidden kisses melt into passion, *both* are haunted by their explosive encounter...

#2924 A COWBOY KIND OF THING

Texas Cattleman's Club: The Wedding • by Reese Ryan

Tripp Nobel is convinced Royal, Texas, is perfect for his famous cousin's wedding. But convincing Dionna Reed, the bride's Hollywood best friend...? The wealthy rancher's kisses soon melt her icy shell, but will they be enough to tempt her to take on this cowboy?

#2925 RODEO REBEL

Kingsland Ranch • by Joanne Rock

With a successful bull rider in her bachelor auction, Lauryn Hamilton's horse rescue is sure to benefit. But rodeo star Gavin Kingsley has his devilish, bad boy gaze on *her*. The good girl. The one who's never ruled by reckless passion—until now...

#2926 THE INHERITANCE TEST

by Anne Marsh

Movie star Declan Masterson needs to rehabilitate his playboy image fast to save his inheritance! Partnering with Jane Charlotte—the quintessential "plain jane"—for a charity yacht race is a genius first step. If only there wasn't a captivating woman underneath Jane's straightlaced exterior...

#2927 BILLIONAIRE FAKE OUT

The Image Project • by Katherine Garbera

Paisley Campbell just learned her lover is a famous Hollywood A-lister... and she's expecting his baby! Sean O'Neill knows he's been living on borrowed time by keeping his identity secret. Can he convince her that everything they shared was not just a celebrity stunt?

#2928 A GAME OF SECRETS

The Eddington Heirs • by Zuri Day

CEO Jake Eddington was charged with protecting his friend's beautiful sister from players and users. And he knows *he* should resist their chemistry too...but socialite Sasha McDowell is too captivating to ignore—even if their tryst ignites a scandal...

Get 4 FREE REWARDS!

We'll send you 2 FREE Books plus 2 FREE Mystery Gifts.

FREE
Value Over
$20

Both the **Harlequin® Desire** and **Harlequin Presents®** series feature compelling
novels filled with passion, sensuality and intriguing scandals.

YES! Please send me 2 FREE novels from the Harlequin Desire or Harlequin
Presents series (gifts are worth about $10 retail). After
receiving them, if I don't wish to receive any more books, I can return the
shipping statement marked "cancel." If I don't cancel, I will receive 6 brand-
new Harlequin Presents Larger-Print books every month and be billed just
$6.30 each in the U.S. or $6.49 each in Canada, a savings of at least 10% off
the cover price, or 6 Harlequin Desire books every month and be billed just
$5.05 each in the U.S. or $5.74 each in Canada, a savings of at least 12%
off the cover price. It's quite a bargain! Shipping and handling is just 50¢ per
book in the U.S. and $1.25 per book in Canada.* I understand that accepting
the 2 free books and gifts places me under no obligation to buy anything. I can
always return a shipment and cancel at any time by calling the number below.
The free books and gifts are mine to keep no matter what I decide.

Choose one: ☐ **Harlequin Desire**   ☐ **Harlequin Presents Larger-Print**
                        (225/326 HDN GRJ7)   (176/376 HDN GRJ7)

Name (please print)

Address   Apt. #

City   State/Province   Zip/Postal Code

Email: Please check this box ☐ if you would like to receive newsletters and promotional emails from Harlequin Enterprises ULC and
its affiliates. You can unsubscribe anytime.

Mail to the Harlequin Reader Service:
IN U.S.A.: P.O. Box 1341, Buffalo, NY 14240-8531
IN CANADA: P.O. Box 603, Fort Erie, Ontario L2A 5X3

Want to try 2 free books from another series! Call 1-800-873-8635 or visit www.ReaderService.com.

*Terms and prices subject to change without notice. Prices do not include sales taxes, which will be charged (if applicable) based
on your state or country of residence. Canadian residents will be charged applicable taxes. Offer not valid in Quebec. This offer is
limited to one order per household. Books received may not be as shown. Not valid for current subscribers to the Harlequin Presents
or Harlequin Desire series. All orders subject to approval. Credit or debit balances in a customer's account(s) may be offset by any
other outstanding balance owed by or to the customer. Please allow 4 to 6 weeks for delivery. Offer available while quantities last.

Your Privacy—Your information is being collected by Harlequin Enterprises ULC, operating as Harlequin Reader Service. For a
complete summary of the information we collect, how we use this information and to whom it is disclosed, please visit our privacy notice
located at corporate.harlequin.com/privacy-notice. From time to time we may also exchange your personal information with reputable
third parties. If you wish to opt out of this sharing of your personal information, please visit readerservice.com/consumerschoice or
call 1-800-873-8635. **Notice to California Residents**—Under California law, you have specific rights to control and access your data.
For more information on these rights and how to exercise them, visit corporate.harlequin.com/california-privacy.

HDHP22R3

HARLEQUIN
PLUS

Announcing a **BRAND-NEW** multimedia subscription service for romance fans like you!

Read, Watch and Play.

Experience the easiest way to get the romance content you crave.

Start your **FREE 7 DAY TRIAL** at
www.harlequinplus.com/freetrial.